THE MORPHING OF INNOCENCE

MICHAEL McCARTHY

Formatting by C. S. Cooper
www.cscooper.com.au

Cover Art by White Rose Publishing Service
www.whiterosepublishingservice.com

Paperback ISBN: 978-1-7638853-0-1
eBook ISBN: 978-1-7638853-1-8

Prologue

Draig, the black Zaurlock belonged to a race of alphawizards that had tyrannically ruled the earth for eons prior to the formation of The Council of Rah. Zaurlocks had possessed extraordinary talents and capabilities, until their powers were curtailed and limited by The Council over one hundred years ago. Draig was, for the first time in many decades, feeling as though he was not achieving anything worthwhile.

He had reached the pinnacle of his restrained powers as the Cardinal Head of his unusually talented race, but he felt that his life had stagnated. He had become jaded and uninterested. He needed more stimulus – more motivation. He had dabbled in the area of morphing animals from one form to another, which held his interest for a while, but he had never morphed a human. That was until he had experimented on his devoted apprentice. It had not gone well.

The rejection by the king for the coveted position as Chief Court Zaurlock had been the final factor that had driven him to seek power beyond this world. He had opened himself up to an unearthly influence, which had certainly made his life more interesting as it increased his powers dramatically, but there had been a price to pay. His mind had not been the same since he had become an agent for the evil one. Something was making him think very differently and he could not stop it. At times his mind ran rampant and he felt he was not fully in control of his actions.

He had become obsessed with an inappropriate degree of revenge against the king for rejecting him as Chief Zaurlock. At first, he had some small insight that he was being unreasonable, but it soon vanished as the feeling was replaced with a lustful passion to repay Henrik at any cost for the manifest transgression committed against him personally.

He had enough acumen to not overtly wreak his vengeance on the king. He would be banished for treason. He had to exact his revenge in a more subtle way. The widowed king had an only daughter whom he loved dearly. She would be his means to bring down the mighty monarch. His innocent pawn used to conquer and destroy a culpable king.

Chapter 1

The palace cat had a more enchanted life than she did. How could the days of a princess be so ordinary and so mediocre? Megan wanted some excitement in her life. She was bored with the routine at the palace. Every day seemed to be the same.

She was in her bed, drifting into that somnolent and comfortable state that she always felt just before sleep came. Uninvited thoughts of how ordinary her life seemed, bubbled up again in her mind. She had so much to be thankful for, so Hilda the maid had told her, but she did not want to be thankful. She wanted some exhilaration and stimulation to cut across the monotony and tedium. It had to be something outrageous and challenging to lift her out of her malaise. She looked around her room at all the beauty and opulence she possessed. She had everything a girl could possibly need, or want. Her room had been specially decorated for her under orders from her father King Henrik. No expense had been spared. If she was to admit it to herself she really liked her room. She was always keen to show it off to her girlfriends when they were allowed to visit. It was her sanctuary, her place of refuge, where she could escape into her own vivid imagination, letting it run free and unabated. She frequently escaped here into her own mind, but even that had not worked lately. She really needed something.

She gazed absently around at the unique character of the

decor in her room, letting her thoughts wander as she did.

The high walls were a very light pink collage of fanciful characters and drawings etched into the plastered surface. There were princesses in golden carriages with magnificent white chargers sweeping across the wall under the high-arched window. The most beautiful set of polished oak shutters used to close out the light and the cold, adorned each side of the arched window. The ceiling was a dome shape divided into six sections, each a different shade of red, from light cerise to darkest vermillion. Each division had a separate story-tale character painted in stimulating pastel shades.

A large chandelier hung from the centrepiece of the dome. It had dozens of ornate candles, which Hilda the maid lit each night and extinguished sometime after Megan had fallen asleep. The door was made of solid oak. It had a crystal lever latch that shone brightly in the light which reflected off the candelabra sitting on the mirrored dresser. Megan would sit for hours at her dresser, just looking at her own image and trying on all her many exotic pieces of jewellery. Her father had gotten these for her from all over the known world. The dresser was a special gift from her uncle for her eighth birthday. It had mirrors hinged on either side of the centre glass, which she could move to gain the best view of herself as she played dress up. She especially liked to choose elegant clothes from her well-stocked wardrobe and dress like a queen. It reminded her of her mother. She kept a picture of her displayed in pride of place on the mantelpiece over the large log fireplace. She dearly missed her mother, who had been prematurely taken by the sickness when Megan was just five years old. Nobody could ever fill the need she had for her mother's love and affection. Her father had tried his best, but it was not the same. There were times when she longed for her mother's embrace. Things that she needed to say, that she could not share with anyone else were left unsaid. She still awoke some nights weeping and not knowing why. She had come to accept that life was not always kind, and that fate did not seek her blessing.

Her Favorite piece of furniture was her bed. It was very large for just one little girl. The most expensive cover shone with elaborately embroidered swirls of miniature clear sparkling diamonds and dazzling white pearls. The ornate bed head dominated the room. It was heavily quilted in jade colour silken fabric, which was speckled with the reddest ruby studs adorning the cushioned upholstery. In the centre was a large jewel. It was fashioned with every sort of precious gemstone imaginable. It irradiated a purple shimmer as the light caught it from different angles. Set just above her head, she could lie back in bed and see the light refracting through the jewel cluster, sending shafts of different colour beams radiating off in every direction. It was a special present her father the king had given her when she had turned ten on her last birthday. She really felt that she was fortunate. As the only child of the king, she was always getting beautiful gifts from her father, or one of their wealthy relatives. These things she was reflecting on as she felt herself sinking again into the tranquil pool of slumber.

Unexpectedly, she came fully awake, and all her senses tingled with an uncanny, mysterious feeling of apprehension. She sensed something strange and foreboding. Tension enveloped her mind and body; so much so, that she felt she could not undo invisible bonds that inexplicably and suddenly seemed to hold her captive. She clenched her teeth, and her fists, as a shadow of fear permeated the atmosphere. The air vibrated with waves of sheer magical power, and it felt to her like it was dousing its sinister contents over the very essence of her being. The walls seemed to lose focus and became hazy and blurred. She looked up and forced her mind to concentrate on the arched window. It was open wide. Hilda had not closed the shutters. The mystical energy was coming from the open window, and seemingly from the full moon beyond. She desperately reached out into her thoughts for some assurance. Wasn't her room high up in the palace bell tower, and supposedly safe and secure?

A beam of splintered light, impregnated with swirls of sparkling flecks and spirals entered her room and thrust its force directly at the large purple jewel. The jewel did not shatter but reflected the light back filling the room with an illumination so brilliant, that Megan had to close her eyes tightly. A series of grotesque screeches and hoarse shrieks muffled the ominous words which were voiced amidst the cacophony.

"I have power over you." The words repeated over and over many times before melding back into the hideous clamour and then fading away completely.

Once the words and the din ceased, Megan ventured a quick look, gingerly opening one eye at a time. The light had dissipated as quickly as it had come. The room looked like it had before anything had happened, except for the jewel, which still pulsated with magic and glowed with a most unusual and ethereal light. Megan had never seen anything as wraithlike and eerie as this before. She just lay there dumbfounded and amazed at the unbelievable thing that had just occurred. It took her some time to settle her tense nerves and stressed emotions. She had not even been able to scream for help.

Her mind was now far too active and would not allow her to sleep. She got up out of bed and sat down at her mirrored dresser. She stole a look back at the purple jewel. The light was fading and the pulsations seemed to be less frequent, but it was still alive with the power of whatever had struck it. She turned her attention momentarily to the reflection looking back at her from the mirror. She noticed that she still had a look of fear and trepidation on her young face. She was after all only ten years old. This did not happen to her every day. She calmed herself, took a deep breath and continued to look at herself.

She was tall for her age and had long blonde hair platted into two pigtails. Her eyes were the brightest blue with flecks of violet. Her skin was clear, and she had just a few freckles on her nose and cheeks. Despite the unusual events that had just occurred, she still managed to think to herself that she was really a nice-looking princess.

She wondered what the magic was all about. She was proud of herself, in that she was able to force her mind and emotions not to worry unduly about the visitation. As there had been a lot of supernatural occurrences happening in the kingdom lately, her father had said for her to be careful, especially when the moon was really round. Because of the strange happenings in the realm, the king gave her a special necklace to wear in case she ever needed to call upon Sagent Nah, the white Zaurlock for help. But she had been warned not to use it unless she was really in need. Hanging from the necklace, was a heart-shaped locket which, when opened would release a Halopod. This little messenger being would go directly to Sagent Nah's Keep, and bring him back to help her. The king had explained to Megan, that a Halopod was a small amorphous magical life form no larger than a pear. It appeared to be transparent but had a definite facial structure with small intelligent eyes. It could empathize and understand Megan's thoughts, words, and intentions. Sagent Nah had created the Halopod, especially for Megan's protection. She liked to call it Gemma. She wondered why she had not had the presence of mind to call her this time.

She got up and went over to the arched window. Standing on the step under it, she peered hesitantly out into the night sky. The brightness coming through the aperture, illuminated her face as she observed the full round moon in the night sky. It appeared oddly brighter, as though it too had experienced something freakish that night.

The drama seemed to have passed for the moment, and it was getting very late. Megan made her way back to her bed. She tried to think about why the light had come, but for some reason, she could not focus her thoughts. A weird desensitizing feeling overcame her. She lapsed into a very lethargic state, and before she realized it, she was fast asleep.

* * *

As the sun's rays shone through the arched window and the first crimson shafts of the morning light permeated her room, Megan slowly began to rouse. She woke up with a start, almost expecting to see something frightening in her room.

Her instantly active mind went to the momentous events of the night before. What had really taken place? Did it actually happen at all, or did she imagine the whole thing? There had been numerous reports of many unusual magical episodes occurring throughout the Eastlands. Some of the chilling tales, of people being morphed into beasts and all sorts of other creatures, caused Megan to shudder at the very thought of it.

She stretched her arms and, raising her hands up over her head gave a big yawn.

A strange beastly sound issued forth from somewhere very, very close to her.

Megan quickly brought her hands back under the blankets. She wanted to scream out to Hilda but did not move, for she feared that something fierce was in her room. It might attack her if she did. She was afraid to even open her eyes and kept them tightly closed. As she felt her own hands under the blankets, they felt odd and hairy. Immediately she separated them and tried to use them to clutch the sheets tightly. She suspected that what she had touched was in fact, her own hand. Thinking that she had made a horrible mistake, she bravely tried once more. She withdrew her hand in disbelief. Just as she had suspected, she felt hair again.

She forced herself to lift her hand up in front of her face.

She tentatively opened her eyes and looked. She was amazed to see a brown furry paw with a long-curved claw-type fingernails. She thought that she must be still asleep and having a bad dream prompted by the last night's unearthly events. She was mistaken. This was real. She did not want to touch the furry paw, so she wiggled her fingers to see if it would respond … it did.

She mustered her courage and slipped her feet over the side of the bed. Her feet were also hirsute with long curved nails and looked more like the paws of an animal. She wobbled on the balls of her small feet as she stood. Something was definitely not right. Taking hold of her ragged senses and trying not to panic, she moved awkwardly across the floor to the mirrored dresser.

Peeking around the edge of the mirror she was shocked again to see, what looked like a large brown fox staring back at her. She jumped back from the image. What had happened to her? She surely could not be a fox. She was a princess. The thing she had feared most had come upon her. She had been morphed.

There was a loud rap at the door. Megan quickly looked for a place to hide.

"Good morning Princess Megan," the voice of Hilda the maid sounded from the other side of the door, "Can I come in?"

Megan tried to say, "Just a moment." But only whines came out.

She quickly crawled and squirmed her awkward new body under the bed, and only just remembered to pull in her bushy tail as Hilda stepped through the door.

"Where are you, sweetheart?" Hilda looked around the empty room thinking perhaps that Megan had already gone down early for her breakfast. She thought that was unusual, but absently went about her duties.

Megan dared not answer her. She breathed hard but managed to keep herself hidden and quiet so that she would not be detected. Hilda would only panic if she saw a fox in her bedroom.

It felt to Megan like the maid was taking forever to tidy her room before she finally went out again. She closed the door behind her.

Relieved, Megan slipped out from her hiding place and ventured one more timid look into the mirror. There was no doubt about it. She was a fox dressed in a little girl's pyjamas. She even started to feel uncomfortable standing upright and had trouble balancing while standing on two legs. In fact, she felt a sense of relief when she dropped down on all fours. What was going on?

She reasoned to herself that she could not stay in the palace. If her father the king saw her as a fox, of course, he would not know it was her, and he would send the guards after her. She had to think of a way to get out of the palace and into the safety of the forest, where she could at least find refuge and think of some sort of plan.

She had to tell her father somehow. On her dresser, there was paper and an ink pen which she used to practice her writing. She would write a note telling her father that she had been morphed into a fox and that she had fled into the forest until he could send help. But, when she went over to the dresser and tried to pick up the pen with her paw, she realized that it wasn't going to work. She could not even hold a pen. She quickly abandoned the idea.

She walked on all fours over to the step under the window. It was difficult, but she managed to stretch up on her back legs and peer out through the window. She could not see over the sill but remembered that it was a long way down to the ground. Much too far to jump, and she could not climb down the outside of the tower as a fox. The only real way out was to escape through the front doors of the palace.

She moved to her bedroom door and, clumsily using her paw to pull the lever latch down, opened it. She stuck her big brown head out through the door opening. Much to her chagrin, her ears flicked involuntarily in a fox-like manner as she looked searchingly down the long hallway toward the staircase. She looked first one way and then, turning her head around she sniffed the air as she looked down all the way to the other end.

Hilda was nowhere to be seen. The hallway was empty.

She withdrew back inside her room. She quickly took off her pyjamas, using her teeth to drag and tear the clothes from her vulpine body. A fox had no need of clothing. She furtively slipped out into the wide hallway and silently padded her way toward the massive staircase leading to the lower levels, and to the front door, and to freedom. She felt her ears stick straight up in alertness, and her bushy tail flick as she moved stealthily forward.

Just as she was about to place her foot on the first step, she heard a loud scream of alarm coming from behind. Hilda was yelling now at the top of her high-pitched voice. "A fox … there is a fox in the palace. Help, someone help."

Megan seized the moment and leapt down the stairway. She was amazed at how fast she could actually run as a fox. Four legs certainly helped. She bounded down the stairs taking two at a time. Reaching the foyer, she took two more steps and then leapt fully at the chest of one of the palace sentinels standing guard at the huge front doors. He went careering backwards, and with a mighty thump, he smashed into the doors, forcing them open with the impact of his fall. Megan continued on over the top of the hapless guard, and out through the open doors. She bounded at full speed over the moat bridge and into the forest, before the guard could regain his footing and raise the alarm.

Chapter 2

She kept bounding along the forest trail with long open strides. As the trail became narrow and twisted, the line of trees at the forest edge on either side gradually changed shape and appeared to close in on her. It was no longer welcoming but took on a sinister foreboding quality, which made Megan feel afraid. She had no choice but to continue and go deeper. She found herself in the most remote part of the Hajus Woods. Her father had warned her not to venture into this part of the forest, but she felt that at the moment this was oddly her safest place. She reasoned that if no one else dared to go there, she would at least be left alone to figure out her very odd predicament. The Hajus Woods had a bad reputation for being a place where sinister things occurred. Even plants and trees grew differently there. As she walked warily along, she noticed the twisted gnarly branches on the trees which looked to her like they were writhing in pain. They entwined themselves around each other in a death-like strangle, interlocking at their tops to form a thick sinewy canopy above. It almost completely blocked out the life-giving sunshine. It was said, that some people, after venturing into these woods never came out again.

She did not experience tiredness. Nervous energy kept her alert. She felt that she could run all day. As she got deeper into the unsanctified woods, the light began to grow fainter, and the narrow trail became darker and more indistinct. It was almost impossible for her to see ahead. Eventually, it became so dark and perilous that she had to stop completely.

Sitting back down to rest on her haunches, she felt her long tongue involuntarily come lolling out of her mouth. It exuded a viscous loop of saliva, which dribbled down onto her chest. She thought it was disgusting, but could do nothing about it. She tried to exclaim aloud her revulsion, but of course only whines and growls came out of her mouth. Would she ever become accustomed to being a fox? The thought dismayed her.

"You may in time," a deep resonate voice echoed through the woods, startling her out of her reverie.

She spun around to see where the ominous voice came from. There, on the shadowy woodland trail stood a large, dark, sinister looking being. She could see his silhouette clearly because of the green aura which surrounded him. It illuminated the grimness of his features giving them a luminous, greenish glow. His face and hands were much whiter, in stark contrast to the darkness of his dress. The magic emanated from his being in short bolts of pure dark power, shooting out in all directions, and adding to the malevolent vibe surrounding him.

He was tall. He towered higher than her father by a full head and shoulders. He was dressed in a long black mantle adorned with flecks which looked like magical dust, sporadically glowing and fizzling as the cape was ruffled by the wind. All his clothes were black. His long boots extended to his knees. He wore a snakeskin mask over his intense eyes and prominent nose, enhancing his overall appearance of evil. In his hand, was a long staff which had strange markings and runes all over it. Its end had a three-pronged spearhead, which pulsed with mystical energy, glowing intermittently in red and yellow like a flame, but not burning. His facial expression was the epitome of malice and spitefulness, and when he smiled it showed one of his front teeth had rotted out, and was completely missing.

Megan was shaken, but she did not show it. Was she becoming accustomed to the appearance of strange and disturbing things? She oddly thought that this wicked-looking being might even be able to help her in her most unusual situation.

Mustering her resolve she started to speak. A strange whining sound came out of her mouth, but surprisingly, she understood herself clearly. Speaking in fox language, she boldly blurted out a challenge to the uncanny, frightening figure before her.

"Who are you, malevolent one?"

He did not react immediately but appeared to understand her, which did not surprise Megan. He looked as though he had strong magic, and, understanding other forms of language would not a problem to him.

"An interesting choice of words Princess Megan, and you have only learnt that big one yesterday from your royal tutor." He waited again for his revelation to dawn on her. He had been secretly observing her already. "I will deem to answer your question only because I choose to. I am Draig, the black Zaurlock and I rule here in the Hajus Woods, and soon, I will rule everywhere in realm of Eastlands. Surely you have heard of me." He said questioningly as he stepped closer to Megan.

"You can understand me?"

"Of course I can," he scoffed arrogantly, "I am Draig, and I can also read your thoughts. So be very careful with the things you think about me, or I will know." His warning took on a threatening tone as he stepped even closer to her.

"Can you help me please, I've been morphed into a fox by some depraved power, and I am really a princess," she said, almost crying as she spoke pleadingly, "My father King Henrik will reward you well, if you help me and keep me from harm."

"Is that so … actually I need nothing from *your father*," his menacing emphasis gave her some cause for concern. "In fact, it was I who morphed you into a fox. Through my resplendent power, I made the moon shaft connect to the purple jewel on your bed." He glared at her, gauging her reaction to his brash admission.

Megan was shocked and abhorred by his arrogance and disregard for her plight. So much so, that she began to whine furiously. She was outraged, and she let the anger rise within her as she spat the words at him.

"Why did you do it, you are a bad Zaurlock. My father will hear of this and he will not be happy. He will hunt you down and punish you. You will not be able to hide from him."

Before he could frame an answer, Megan darted deftly around him and ran as fast as she could back up the narrow woodland trail, away from the darkness and toward the light. She could hear the Zaurlock's raucous laughter, echoing and fading behind her as she fled.

* * *

She ran until she could run no more. Exhaustion was catching up with her quickly. Taking a fearful look behind her, she furtively slipped off the main trail. She sat down behind a large trunked tree to rest and try to figure out just where she was and what she would do next. She felt completely alone and forsaken. The feeling overwhelmed her, and she began to weep. Deep sobs racked her body.

"What is troubling you?" a kindly male voice came from just behind her, startling her in the silence.

Megan jumped to her feet, fearing the worst. She turned quickly around, not knowing what to expect, only to find another fox standing quietly in front of her, its bushy tail wagging slowly in a non-aggressive way.

"Umm, I am not sure if I believe this, but I just clearly heard what you said," She stammered anxiously, "I must be able to understand fox language?"

"Well yes, of course you can understand fox language; after all, you are a fox, aren't you?" Her new visitor seemed to be amused at her lack of insight, and his stating of the obvious.

Megan started to explain her recent dramatic change but stopped short, as she did not think her story would be credible, even to this obviously intelligent animal who could talk back to her. Would the fox believe her if she said that she was really a princess? She was not convinced.

Fortunately, the gregarious fox spoke first. "My name is Rasita, what is your name?"

"Ahh, my name is Megan," she noted that his voice was deep and strong, and it gave her a feeling of confidence in him.

She was still amazed that she could speak some unknown animal language and communicate with a fox so easily. He did not share the same fascination. It all seemed quite normal to him.

Rasita continued. "Have you got creature force?"

Megan had never heard of it before. She did not really want to know about any kind of extraneous force. She just wanted to be normal again, but her curiosity urged her to ask. It may help her situation.

"What is creature force?"

"What is creature force?" his eyebrows lifted as he thought

of the most appropriate explanation for her. "Well it's what some foxes and some other animals have, that is like the magic that some humans possess. It is good magic, and we use it only for doing good deeds."

Megan thought about what Rasita had just said. She desperately needed a friend and some real help, if she was ever going to be normal again.

She looked him straight in the eye, still gauging his sincerity and looking for possible ulterior motives. She had lost trust, and now she felt she had to be more careful about to whom she revealed her innermost secrets. She had just met Rasita.

"Rasita, I do not know you very well, but I am in a lot of trouble, would you help me?"

"If I can help I will?" Again, she stared deeply into his eyes, searching and testing his earnestness.

"Well, I am not sure where to start, but I am just going to say it." She blurted out her statement with obvious relief at being able to verbalize her plight to someone. "I am a human princess and not a fox." She sat back down again, still not convinced that she had made the right decision.

"I already knew that," said Rasita with a vulpine smile. "I could sense that you were a human as soon as I saw you. It is not by chance that we meet this day. Don't worry it will only last for one day." His confidence lifted her spirits.

"Really, how do you know that, I thought I was permanently changed?"

"Well, I know a little something about this. Once the sun goes down, you can change back into a princess. You will have to use a strong measure of creature force, and be back in your bed for it to unravel, otherwise the spell cannot be broken." His eyes averted when he said the last words, making Megan wonder why.

"And remember this," Rasita added with a sober look on his face. "When you are back in your bed, and the sun goes down, say this magic word which I can only whisper into your ear. Once you say it, the spell will start to break, and you will soon be a princess once more."

He put his nose close to Megan's ear and whispered something. Megan nodded her head locking the word into her memory. Could it be true, that she now knew a way back out of Draig's wicked snare? She needed to know if Rasita really knew the type of power that had done this.

"Have you ever heard of the black Zaurlock Draig?" She came straight to the point.

At the mention of his name, Rasita flinched markedly and when he spoke again, his voice was quivering. "Yes, I have. The Zaurlock's are a race of particularly strong and gifted alphawizards who have extraordinary powers and who live for centuries. You should stay well clear of Draig. Methinks it was he who morphed you into a fox, am I right?"

"Yes, you are right, I just saw him in the Hajus Wood, and he told me that he was responsible for this, and that he meant to do it." She looked down at her body as she spoke. "Do you think he can stop me from changing back?"

"He is not able to stop the rehumanizing, unless he somehow stops you from getting back to your bed by sundown tonight. He may have been the cause of it happening in the first place, but he cannot prevent you from returning to your human form. You must however, do all three things that I have told you." He seemed saddened by his own words.

To Megan, he appeared to know exactly what he was talking about.

"How could he do this to me? Once I change back to a princess, I am going to tell my father the king about what he has done." Megan's voice took on a wounded tone.

"I need to tell you something young Megan … I was once human as well."

His blunt revelation came as a shock to her. She was immediately intent in what he had to say.

He continued wistfully with a sense of sadness clouding his carefully spoken words. "I was once a young man of only twenty years of age when I first began as Draig's understudy. He taught me, and trained me in the magical arts, so that one day I too, would be a great alphawizard. I was born with a predilection which some call 'the gift.' I worshiped and admired him unreservedly. I gave up my heritage to become his apprentice. My father disowned me. But I was certain that this was what I wanted to do with my life. We worked closely together every day, sharing the successes and failures of his experiments into the ethereal world, especially on the subject of morphing."

Rasita lowered his head and had trouble continuing. He swallowed hard, and fought to regain his poise.

Megan waited patiently allowing him to recover his composure. Even at the early stage of her morphing experience she could empathize with him.

With his heavy heart still influencing his words, he resumed his evocative story. "We changed many animals into other forms, with varying success in changing them back to their original form. But, we had never morphed a human." He stopped as if to emphasize the point.

She could sense where this was heading but did not comment, allowing him to reveal his secret to her in his own time.

"I loved and respected him like no other, and when he asked me to take part in his most intrepid and daring experiment, I could not refuse him. I said, that I thought it was too early to attempt, but he was insistent." Small teardrops welled up in his eyes and started to run down his face as he continued his poignant tale.

"As you can see I am still a fox." He finished his tragic tale by turning his face from her.

His last statement frightened Megan. Was she too going to be destined to remain a fox? Desperately, but with as much decorum as she could manage, she asked. "Why could you not be changed back?"

He turned back to face her and noted her look of genuine concern. "We did not know as much as we do now about the reversal of the process. It was too early for us to be experimenting on humans. When I was morphed, the deadline of one day was not known, and I naively passed it, without realizing the dire consequences."

"How can you be so sure that it will work with me?" She felt selfish in asking, but she was also driven by self-preservation.

"I know because I hold part of the key." Rasita looked at her directly in the eye. "I have been waiting for this moment for a very, very long time. It is the combination of both our creature forces which is necessary to bring … only one of us back."

The impact of his words fell heavily on Megan. If she understood him correctly, he was saying that only one of them could return. One would have to sacrifice their irreplaceable creature force, in order for the other one to make it back. She was immediately on guard. Did he intend to use her creature force for himself? Was he really the enemy, and a present danger to her?

He seemed to sense her trepidation and fear. "Please, Megan, do not think that I am considering what the fearful look on your face is imagining. I have been in this form for many years now, and I have got quite accustomed to it. Besides, there is the prophecy to consider."

"Prophecy?" she gave him a questioning look. "What prophecy?"

He responded quickly hearing the urgency in her voice. "Years ago, in my studies with Draig, he uncovered an old book of prophecies. One of the texts spoke of the renting of the shroud between earth and deep earth. It spoke also of a chosen one, who would be persecuted without cause, but would be the one to right the wrong. She would be innocent." Rasita finished his short dissertation and looked straight into Megan's eyes. "I believe that it is you of which the prophecy speaks. You are the innocent, who has been chosen to right the wrong. I believe that the proclaiming of this prophecy is very close, so you see that I cannot, and would not, stand in the way of your returning to your human form."

She did not know how to respond to his words. Surely she was not anything like what he was saying. Nor did she want to be the savior of the world, or anything half as grand. She was just a girl, who wanted a normal life, enjoying her childhood. She was no heroine like she had read about in the story tales. Had she not spent time sitting with her father as he presided over matters of court, she would have no real understanding of what Rasita was talking about. She was very mature for her age and understood sophisticated concepts usually reserved for one much older. Understanding did not relieve her of the burden of what he had said. Was she really to be used for a task of such magnitude? Surely there were better choices than a ten-year-old girl. She longed for the comfort of her father's embrace.

It suddenly dawned on her the sacrifice that Rasita was making. He was setting aside his own needs to make way for her restoration. The nobility of this act touched her heart. "You are truly a decent and honourable person Rasita," she called him a person out of respect.

She moved closer to him, and as best as she could manage she embraced him rubbing her head and neck on his. "Your sacrifice will not be forgotten. I will do everything in my power to bring you back."

Rasita acknowledged her commitment with a pensive nod of

his head. It was as if he had already accepted and resolved the issue in his mind, that he would never again be human. He would never know the love of a woman. In his time as a fox, he had not been able to assimilate with other foxes. Megan's coming gave him a short glimmer of hope, that finally fate had dealt him a hand that he could use to ease his loneliness. He could at least have a sensible conversation with her, but now he was constrained by his sense of nobility to give her the opportunity to return. He did not fit anywhere. He would live out his shortened life span as a fox, and then pass to hopefully somewhere better. Fate had dealt him a hand which he could do nothing about.

"Sometimes in life, we are called upon to do our part for the greater good." He humbly dismissed any further discussion on the subject and turned his attention to matters at hand.

Megan knew that Draig was devious and beguiling, and could understand fox language, so she whispered quietly to Rasita.

"It is getting late, and if I am to save the world, I really need to be changed back to a princess, so let's get started." The attempt at humour was not lost on Rasita. He smiled briefly in his vulpine way, then looking seriously again as he said. "Indeed, but you have to follow exactly what I say to do."

She nodded her agreement and understanding as they sat opposite each other. They raised their front paws, and put them together balancing each other. Rasita said some magic invocation that she did not understand. Megan felt a shimmering of ethereal waves all around her. She experienced a sense of weightlessness, and as she looked closely at her paws they began to fade from sight. She could see them disappearing in front of her eyes.

"What's happening to me?" She began to panic at the unexpected spontaneous result.

"Worry not," Rasita assured her in his calm and comforting voice, "it is acceptable, this is what is supposed to happen. We use our combined power to infuse you with all my creature force. I am putting a protection shield about you which is making you invisible. It will help you to get back to the palace, unseen."

She calmed herself as she acknowledged his logical explanation.

When they were done Rasita moved back and said, "This is

good, I cannot see you anymore. Now you will be safe to get back into the palace, and into your bed, before the sun goes down."

Megan tested his words by moving from side to side in front of him.

"Are you sure nobody can see me?"

Rasita heard her voice, but could not see her at all. He showed a big toothy smile.

"I am sure. You are completely invisible."

Megan said a brief but meaningful goodbye, and thanked him sincerely for his unselfish forfeit of freedom. The gesture seemed totally inadequate, but she had to say something to him. She secretly vowed again to herself, that if it were at all possible, she would do all she could to help him to regain his human form. She felt a twinge of guilt that he was being left behind, but she was aware that she must act swiftly, or she too would be a victim of a morphing gone wrong. She started off down the woodland trail, and Rasita noticed only her footprints being left in the dust as she walked away.

* * *

She was learning quickly how to move her vulpine body to achieve the most speed. She stretched out her legs in full stride and was making good ground. Her mind was still mulling over the sweet and selfless act that she had just witnessed. Rasita had given his life for her. She felt a fondness for him that she could not quite understand. It was not just gratitude or even admiration. It was something else. Her thoughts were interrupted by the sight which confronted her on the trail ahead. Draig himself stood with his back toward her. She slowed her pace to a walk and tried to make her heavy breathing less noticeable.

He did not seem to notice her as she approached warily. He was busy conjuring some sort of hex. Even though she was invisible, she walked very deliberately and carefully, so as not to alert him to her presence.

She was almost past him when he said gleefully.

"What are these then, fox footprints, appearing all by themselves?"

Megan froze and did not move a muscle. She looked around her for some way of escape. Beside her was a large fallen tree.

She noiselessly leaped up onto it and began to move carefully along its trunk. She stopped momentarily and looked behind her to make sure no footprints were showing. She gradually got further away from the searching Zaurlock.

With an ugly grin on his face, the Zaurlock skulked around looking for her. His hands were out in front of him, and he took giant exaggerated steps like he was playing a grotesque game of hide and seek. He looked here, and there, and with a strange lilt in his voice he said.

"Where are you Megan? I know you are there."

She knew he could detect her thoughts. He had told her as much. So she did her best to make her thoughts blank, and she tried not to project them so that he could not read them.

Fortunately, he went off looking in the wrong direction. She jumped off the very end of the tree trunk and escaped down the trail, running as fast as she could without causing the dust to rise in her wake.

Panting heavily from the tension and the fear, she continued to run toward the palace.

Meanwhile, back on the woodland trail, Draig had stopped his search and was standing still, thinking to himself. He was certain that it was Megan the fox making the footprints. But where would her logical destination be?

"Ah," he said out aloud when inspiration came to him in a flash. "Of course, she is heading for the palace."

He immediately conjured a transportation spell which he rarely used, and switched his location to the moat bridge at the palace to await her arrival.

He did not want to be pestered by the palace guards with their annoying challenges, so he hid himself behind one of the large scrubby plants that grew alongside the palace moat.

Soon Megan came bounding along. She could not wait to be across the bridge and into the safety of the palace. Her father would know what to do. She would tell him everything.

She propped to a sudden stop. The reality of her situation dawned on her. She could not tell him anything until she was changed back. Foxes cannot speak Eastlander tongue, and there was always the danger of their not knowing who she was, and killing her by mistake. She had forgotten that she was invisible and could not be seen.

She looked up into the sky above. The sun was quickly going

down. She had to hurry. Time was running out.

"Going somewhere?" Draig appeared from nowhere, and stood smugly on the rough stone coping at the edge of the moat.

Draig could not see her, but he must have heard her breathing heavily from her exertion as she ran up to the moat bridge.

He laughed loudly as he sent a magical bolt of Zaurlock's fire across in front of her. The fire streamed from his hand in long blue strands, spiralling and crackling as it went. The ground was scorched and burning where the bolt made its impact. Megan was prevented from continuing any further. She did not want to get hurt. She realized that being invisible would not prevent her from being burned. The flames in front of her were rising up higher. They did not seem to burn out but increased in intensity as if they had intentions of their own.

Judging her position by the footprints she had made in the dust, he continued the stream of Zaurlock's fire coming from both his hands now. It formed a fiery circle around her. He laughed more as he performed his nasty act, for he knew that she was trapped.

The fire burned higher all around her. She could feel the intense heat starting to singe her fur. The protection shield that Rasita had put in place was working, but she did not know for how long. She was aware that her time was running out. If she did not reach her bed by nightfall she would have to remain a fox forever. But more importantly, how was she going to get out of this fire trap right now? How could she escape his ghastly clutches? She almost gave up hope when she remembered her locket. In all the confusion, she had again forgotten to call upon her helper.

Megan had not even thought to check if the locket had gone with her when she was morphed. She found it hard to use her paws to feel if the locket was still around her neck. Her eyes stung with the heat and the acrid smell that came from the intense circle of flame surrounding her.

How was she going to open the locket to call Sagent Nah, the white Zaurlock to help her? An idea dropped from nowhere into her racing mind. Perhaps she could use creature force? She now had Rasita's as well. She was not sure if it would work, but at the moment she had one chance, and she was in the form of a fox so she decided to give it a try. She had little choice.

She concentrated hard, closing her eyes and blocking out the closeness and the danger of the fire trap raging around her. She silently prayed to the Holy One for His intervention. She clearly saw in her imagination the locket still hanging around her neck opening up.

Gemma the Halopod appeared before her eyes. She was unaffected by the flames and looked this time like a curl of white smoke with purple and blue streaks moving into different colours inside it. Small, kind eyes were visible within the smoky transparent being.

"What is your command, Princess Megan?" She asked in perfect fox language.

"Go quickly to Sagent Nah at the white Zaurlock's Keep, and summon him to help me right now."

Gemma moved so quickly that she seemed to disappear instantly.

Almost as quickly the shimmering form of Sagent Nah appeared standing outside the flames. He looked very similar to Draig, but he had a long flowing white beard and everything about him was white, except for his eyes, which were bright blue.

He summed up the situation in an instant and spun around unsheathing and raising his shining sword as he turned. From the blade came an almighty gust of Zaurlock's chillier wind. Its force all but extinguished the flame completely. The burnt ground was left smoking, where the flame had been just moments before.

Draig immediately tried to reignite the fire, but Sagent Nah swung his sword again. This time the chiller wind directed itself toward Draig, and formed into a huge fist-shaped gust, blowing straight at him. It hit him full force in the chest and sent him sprawling onto the hard ground before he could cast another spell. The force of it continued to buffet him until he lost balance and fell backward into the murky water of the moat.

Gemma the Halopod reappeared floating before Megan. Her small eyes seemed to look into hers even though she was still invisible. It looked as though she was nodding her head reassuringly, and saying it was all right now. Gemma returned to the open locket around Megan's furry neck, and it clipped closed by itself.

Sagent Nah stood directly in front of her. He seemed to know exactly where she was. On his face, he wore a kindly smile. He let his shining sword slide easily back into its scabbard. All around him, the air was still moving in rhythmic waves from the raw power that came from him.

"Megan, what have you done to upset my brother the black Zaurlock?" He sounded concerned that she had had any sort of contact with his errant older brother.

Megan answered in fox language assuming that Sagent Nah would also be able to understand.

"I did nothing. He had no reason to do what he did." She sounded vulnerable and hurt. She pouted, allowing herself the small indulgence now that she felt a measure of safety.

"Well, you are talking fox language and you are invisible so you must have done something."

"No, I think that he has a grudge against my father and he also thinks he has more power than the king, and perhaps that is why he is picking on me." Her immature logic held some truth to it.

Sagent Nah stroked his long beard thoughtfully as he said, "All right then, I will take you into the palace now and we can see your father."

"Yes let's do it immediately, there is no time to spare." It was almost nightfall as Megan walked quickly over the moat bridge toward the front gate of the palace.

While they walked across the bridge two vengeful eyes watched them from the darkness below.

Chapter 3

"How dare he!" roared King Henrik, as Sagent Nah told him who the perpetrator was, and what he had done to his Princess Megan. "I have forbidden the use of magic for evil purposes. I will send my palace guards to find and arrest Draig, and have the Council of Rah deal with him." Henrik was furious, and it infuriated him more, that he could not even see his precious daughter who stood right in front of him. He was about to launch into another tirade when Nah asked his indulgence.

Megan told Sagent Nah just what she had to do to break the conjurations that held her now as an invisible fox.

He respectfully pointed out to the king that the most important thing to do right now was to get Megan up into her bed before the sun went down. They had no time to waste. Moments counted.

The king frustratingly waved his hand, giving his permission for Megan to go quickly. "We will talk again young lady once you are back to normal and Nah, we will talk also." The last words directed at the white Zaurlock taking on a disapproving tone.

Sagent Nah escorted Megan to her bedroom and left her saying, "Go quickly, you do not have much time. I will guard the palace, and make sure that you are left in peace, to undo the hexes and be morphed back into a human."

Megan sighed in relief as she walked through the door of her bedroom. She closed the door tightly and flipped the lock latch with her paw. She took in the familiar surroundings, and it calmed her greatly. It had been a really taxing day for her, and she felt exhausted. One quick hopeful look in the mirror showed her that yes, she was still invisible.

She looked up at the arched window. The light coming through the aperture was fading fast. She wasted no time in scrambling into her bed. She managed to accommodate her bushy tail in under the sheets. She was so thankful that she had made it. It was nightfall and she was safe in her bed, just in time. Now, what was that magic word that Rasita had told her? Ah yes that's right.

He had told her not to say it out loud, but only to think the word over and over in her mind, while releasing their combined creature force. She followed his implicit instructions and began to release the force while thinking of the word in her mind.

The room seemed to come alive with mysterious vibrations and light shafts, which randomly appeared, and then shot off in all directions, refracting against the walls and ceiling. They caused small explosions of rainbows to appear at the point of impact, and then vanish an instant later. Megan could feel the energy within her changing. It was as if her cells were being stretched and reformed. She looked at her hand to see if it was back. A faint outline was starting to appear. The silhouette became clear and started to solidify toward the centre. It became stronger and stronger until she could see clearly her hand once more.

She was becoming very excited when all of a sudden it stopped. Something was interfering with the undoing. The image of her hand flickered and then faded from sight again.

Out of nowhere, two figures suddenly materialized in her room. They were locked in a fierce battle. Both had their right arm raised, and each shouted incantations and chants at the other. Good and evil were opposed, and no side would concede. They matched mystical forces with none showing a clear advantage. Sagent Nah drew his sword and swung it in a wide arc, barely missing Draig's head. It hit his raised staff instead and shattered it to pieces. In response, a bolt of magical power aimed at Sagent Nah's body flashed from his opponent's closed fist. Moving swiftly in defence, Sagent Nah deftly dodged the attack as the bolt hit the wall, leaving a deep gouge in the plastered surface. He landed a retaliatory blow, bringing his staff down on the other's head with a resounding crunch. The battle raged until finally, Sagent Nah began to burn with a white anger. His whole body emanated the white heat, as he loosed a righteous disabler web against Draig. It wrapped itself around his body many times, continuing to spiral and tighten with each revolution, stalling and frustrating his evil magic powers.

"Keep going with your change Princess Megan, while I can still hold him." Sagent Nah shouted as he continued to concentrate his righteous power toward Draig.

Draig then aggressively loosed a conjuration of magic from his only free hand, which made both he and Sagent Nah fade in and out of sight, and then disappear completely.

Megan did not waste any time but began again immediately to invoke the demorphing procedure. As before, the room filled with the same magical power, and she found herself being gradually transformed back into herself. She hoped that she could fully complete the process without further interruption. Her life as a human depended on it.

After what seemed a long time, the force of the magic began to fade and dissipate. She got up out of bed, and slowly walked over to the mirror, noticing with relief that her feet seemed back to normal, and her balance was no longer a problem. As she peeked nervously around the edge of the mirror, she was overjoyed to see the image of Princess Megan once more.

It was over, she was back.

She was feeling exhausted from all the demanding events of a truly weird day, but before she got into her bed, she made sure the door was locked securely. She went over to the window and stood on the step. Peeking out over the sill, she noticed that the moon was no longer full, but still quite bright in the night sky. She was just about to close the window when she saw a slight movement near the edge of the forest. A fox was sitting there, and looking up at her. Its tail flicked nervously. She was sure it was Rasita. Megan felt a wrenching pang of emotion in her heart seeing him again. For her, he had laid down his chance at freedom.

Even though she was human again, she thought she felt, rather than heard, Rasita talking to her. He was reassuring her that everything was alright now. Could she still understand fox language? She gave him a slow wave, and a smile, as she closed the window tightly. She also closed the shutters, just in case there was any magic afoot again that night.

Back in her warm bed, she drew up the sheets around her neck. She held her locket safely in her hand, as she drifted quietly, into a sweet peaceful and dreamless sleep.

Chapter 4

From his hiding place in the forest, Draig watched the fox. He knew it was Rasita. They had a history together. He had specially selected him again this time, and had taken, and used part of his unique creature force, to morph Megan into fox form. He needed to know why this particular fox was so intent on the palace bell tower. He must have connected with Megan when she was in fox form. That would explain how she was able to undo the spell, without his authority. He needed to know more, so he extended his right hand toward Rasita. He released his HuverWort from its perch, hidden within the opening of his large hanging sleeve.

The HuverWort was a magical pliable life form. It was created by the black Zaurlock to spy on just about anybody, or anything, without them even knowing it was there. About the size of a small bat, it had a single wing only but seemed to be able to manoeuvre itself well through the air. It was able to hover, remaining effortlessly and silently in one spot. The eyes were disproportionately large, and were similar to those of a fly, with dozens of hexagonally shaped sections all over the spherical surfaces. A set of needle-shaped antennae sat above the eyes. It could translate any language, transform itself into any shape or colour, and transmit thoughts back to the Zaurlock, from any distance. Its entire existence had been dedicated to Draig's cause and had been used only to satisfy his evil whims and desires.

It moved noiselessly through the air settling into position above the fox. It began harvesting the animal's thoughts immediately.

No words, or sounds, could be heard coming from Rasita as he looked at the bell tower of the king's palace. As he focused on the arched window, he was unaware that his thoughts were arcing across space.

'Goodbye Megan. Fare well, you are released now from the evil power of the black Zaurlock, and I am so pleased I could help, and that you are again, a human princess. He cannot harm you anymore. Go, and fulfill your destiny.'

With a final despondent flick of his tail, he acknowledged the wave that Princess Megan gave him as he turned and disappeared into the forest.

As Draig listened, his mouth widened into a crooked jagged smile. He spoke aloud to himself. "Good, they think that I was finished when that dull-witted younger brother of mine Sagent Nah got in my way. I was about to stop Megan from breaking my morphing spell. She will come to realize, that I am the one in charge of her destiny."

As he moved his bony hand in a homing signal to recall his HuverWort, he also began devising in his evil mind, a plan of revenge, which again, unfairly included young Megan.

He derived great satisfaction by involving the king's daughter in his plans. He had vowed to repay the lofty King Henrik for choosing his brother Sagent Nah, rather than him, to be the Chief Court Zaurlock.

What better way to get to the king, than through someone he loved so much? It mattered little to him that Megan had done him no wrong. She was merely a weapon for him to use against the king. A means to his ultimate end. It vaguely occurred to him that he might be being unfair to her, but the notion quickly disappeared. He was confronted in his mind with a weird and wonderful drawing, from a force not of this world. It was strangely enticing, and alluring. He probably should not have sought to dabble in that area, but he was bored with his everyday drab existence. In three hundred years, he had done most things, and he needed more stimuli. He needed to dominate the realm. Since he had made his bargain with the evil one, his power had spiked into a scintillating array of new skills. No, he did not regret it at all.

Back to business, he began stroking his shabby black beard as he did when in deep thought; he considered various morphing options for her to suffer. A snake … no he liked snakes too much. What would his next creature morph be? A sly smile parted his dry and cracked lips, as an idea formed up in his devious and beguiling mind.

* * *

At Court Zaurlock's Keep, Sagent Nah sat at his marble desk contemplating the current set of unusual events, which he was now certain were the work of his older brother Draig. His brother had never forgiven him, or the king, for the decision taken to make him Court Chief Zaurlock. Draig had always bettered him, and dominated him, for as long as he could remember. The king's decision had surprised him as much as it had infuriated Draig. His brother was not one to cross. He had a bad streak, which he relished using if anyone was foolish enough to give him reason. At times, Draig did not even need sufficient reason, he would find unjust cause and seemed to relish taking revenge and using his high degree of magic skills to exact his frequently misguided vengeance.

Sagent Nah had, of late, increased the depth and breadth of his own magic. He only practiced preservative magic, whereas his brother only partook in devastative magic, only to be found at the opposite end of the magical continuum. This form of dark magic had been responsible for much of the discord and disruption running through the Eastlands in recent times. As Chief Court Zaurlock, he had better keep a close eye on his brother's movements, especially concerning Megan. The king had been scathing in his criticism of Sagent Nah's lack of diligence with the latest morphing episode involving his daughter.

As a precaution, he did the least he should do and placed a rune deflection shield around Megan's room. This would hopefully prevent a recurrence of the last day's events.

Even with his increased powers, Sagent Nah had trouble containing his brother. The fight last night had proven that. Draig was held in a strong disabler web, but he had somehow still been able to unleash a spell. He dismantled both their beings, into what appeared to be a spectre of minuscule particles, and sucked them out of Megan's room through some sort of portal. They were reformed and ended up on the top of Mount Isnar. All this was done with a spell that the white Zaurlock had never seen before. New magic.

He had laughed as they faced each other on that craggy cliff on Mount Isnar. Draig was gloating as he boasted of his newly found power.

"Try and resist me," he challenged. "My power is greater than yours little brother, and I will have my revenge."

As he laughed louder, the sky opened up its bowels, and torrents of rain fell, stinging their faces. Great claps of thunder followed the jagged lightning strikes, which hit the ground all around them, leaving smouldering scars of burnt earth in their wake.

Sagent Nah had to admit it Draig's power was certainly stronger than it had ever been, and he was much nastier and more vengeful than he could ever remember. He had been fortunate to be able to extract himself from Mount Isnar unscathed.

As he mused over these things, he noticed the hair on the back of his neck standing up. A sure sign that magic was near. He cast his vision around the room. Nothing seemed to be different, but he was certain that something was amiss.

He closed his eyes and engaged his ether vision. A power that even Draig had not mastered. He could see into the spirit realm, and discern the presence of evil. His eyes were closed, but his eyelids glowed with magic power. As he moved his head around the room, two rays of light searched every crevice. The rays focused in on one of the candleholders fixed high up on the wall of his room. Yes, it was not merely a candleholder, it was something else. Something supernatural. It began to reveal itself. Sagent Nah had never seen a being like this before.

Under the scrutiny of his ether vision, it started to transform into its real shape, and feeling the discomfort of the rays, it moved off the wall. It hovered effortlessly in one spot. Its single wing beat silently. As it peered down at him, fleshy shutters came down over its eyes to protect them from the sharpness of the light. As if it sensed something coming, it disappeared in the instant before Sagent Nah cast his disabler web.

* * *

The HuverWort homed back to its master, settling on its perch within his right sleeve. Standing in the mouth of his cavern home, Draig had heard all the thoughts and doubts expressed by his younger brother. He was pleased that the realization was coming to Sagent Nah that his older brother was superior in his power and alphawizardry. It would make him easier to defeat the next time they met.

It was time to put into action the next phase of his plan. King Henrik must be made to suffer. When Draig had almost begged for reconsideration of the position of Chief Court Zaurlock, Henrik had dismissed him without due deliberation. So, what if Draig's magic came from sources not approved by the king and his advisors? Henrik would pay for his arrogance. Unbeknown to him, the mighty king had inadvertently already helped Draig's plans by giving Megan that purple jewel. It had been given by one of Draig's cohorts in mock repayment of a debt to the king. Little did he know that Draig had spelled the jewel to fit his purpose beforehand.

Draig remembered back when he was still welcome at court, a foreigner had bought a black panther to the court to display it in front of the king. Henrik was most impressed with the animal. How would he like to have one of his very own?

A sinister smile widened Draig's mouth as he pictured the scene. The king has ordered that a wild panther, running loose in the kingdom is to be hunted down and captured, only to discover that in reality, he had been hunting his own daughter. Draig smiled again at his nefarious inventiveness and craftiness, He had found that it was easier of late to think of these dastardly schemes. Things just dropped into his mind. He had chosen to tap into a higher power, and it was paying dividends with the additional sense of supremacy he felt. He had made a pact with the evil one. He would be his agent here in the earth. The evil one needed someone in the upper earth to organize his imminent coming. The rent in the shroud was just the beginning. Soon, he would swallow the earth with his host of Heinions. They would pour forth from the pit in mighty legions. As agent, he would be well rewarded for his allegiance. His eyes had glazed over with the euphoria of the prospect.

After some time, he reluctantly returned to the humdrum of reality. He mused on the next development.

He dwelt momentarily on the fox morphing. It was just child's play, an entrée, a Zaurlock's experiment with a new toy. This next experiment was going to be the real test of his morph magic prowess. This time there would be no interference. He was more powerful than Sagent Nah, and the king had only his steel to fight for him. The palace guard was hardly a problem for a black Zaurlock of his standing. Anyway, he was soon to have command of his own army of Heinions from the underworld. Then nothing would stand in his way. He would ascend to the position of supreme commander for the evil one.

Satisfied with his future direction, he turned and walked from the cavern opening to the back recesses of his craggy mountain fortress. He had chosen Mount Isnar for its remoteness and inaccessibility to anyone not possessing particular magical powers. The mountain also had powers of its own which one could draw upon when needed. Draig had lived there for most of his three hundred years on the earth.

In the innermost sanctum of the Zaurlock's abode, Draig started his next depraved and reprehensible conjure.

Chapter 5

Megan woke early. After tentatively checking that she was still human, she laid in bed thinking on the bizarre incidents and freakish happenings of the past day. To her, boring and uninteresting were suddenly very attractive. She was looking forward to spending time over breakfast with her father. There was much she wanted to share with him. The experience with the fox morphing had made her think on many different levels; her future security not being the least. She was concerned that the white Zaurlock had not been able to prevent the morphing from happening. He was supposed to be her protector in the supernatural realm. Her father could only give her protection in the physical realm, and he had done all he could to ensure she was safe. But the battle lay in the spirit world. She needed more. If her father could possibly arrange it, he would do so without a second thought.

She was his only child and he cherished her openly. He always encouraged her to be better in every way, telling her how clever and smart she was, and that he loved her all the way to the moon and back. She was always overjoyed to hear him say that, and loved him in return. They had always enjoyed a very special relationship together.

This was probably the reason why Draig had targeted her, she surmised. Sagent Nah had told her of Draig's unwarranted fury at being rejected as Court Zaurlock. He could not directly act in revenge against the king as he would run the risk of being charged with treason, and exiled from the kingdom. Sagent Nah had said that if that happened, he would lose his powers of magic. The Council of Rah, which had dominion over all matters of enchantment in the Eastlands realm, had decreed it to be so many eons ago. Draig was too crafty and devious to act overtly, but, would at all times choose to act in a sly and deceitful way.

She would discuss this with her father at the first opportunity.

At least she had woken this morning as a normal person. She had to admit to herself though, that the experience of being a fox was, if nothing else, different and interesting. To be able to communicate with Rasita and actually become almost friends with him was quite bizarre. She could be forgiven for thinking that it had not really taken place. The confirmation of the truth of it for her was, when she had seen Rasita out of the window last night, and had felt him talking to her in his reassuring way. Had she retained the ability to communicate with foxes? Or perhaps even other animals. It was uncanny.

She made a mental note to discuss it with her father.

She toyed with the heart shaped locket. She remembered how Gemma the Halopod had appeared when she was in dire need. This was the first time she had actually seen the mysterious little being. How amazing a possession was this? A unique piece of original inventiveness, dedicated to serve and protect her only. It seemed strange that she should feel safety and security from such a small source.

She had been told only to use the Halopod for emergencies, but, she felt that there would be no harm in invoking it now, to draw wisdom and to share thoughts. She placed the locket in her hands using her thumbs to pry the two halves open.

Gemma appeared before her immediately and focused her small bright eyes on her. "Princess Megan what's wrong?" She was immediately alert, and scanned the room for any possible danger that may be lurking.

"Nothing is wrong; I just wanted to speak with you," Megan spoke quickly to calm the vigilant Halopod.

"You know that you are only supposed to call me when you are in trouble." Gemma tried to frown in mock reprimand.

"I know that, but, I am in trouble in a way. I need your wisdom to guide me." Gemma seemed satisfied and was eager to help.

Megan thought carefully before she spoke. "You know that I was transformed into a fox by the black Zaurlock Draig."

"Yes, I do know that. It must have been terrible for you."

"It was not so bad. In fact, I quite enjoyed being with Rasita…"

Megan's reply was cut short as the Halopod dramatically changed colour to a bright red, and cried out urgently. "Quick Megan, I sense danger all around."

Megan could now sense it too. It was happening again. She looked for somewhere to hide, but knew there was nowhere to escape this sort of power. This was magic again, and it was in her room. What happened to the deflection shield that was supposed to be around her as protection? She had no time to consider it anymore as the room burst into celestial activity.

There was a splintering crash, as Sagent Nah hurtled in through the door, leaving it shattered and in pieces on the floor. He immediately sensed the dark enchantment, and raised his right hand, releasing a magical counter force. An aura of white energy surrounded him, as the force for good emanated forth and sought to match the shadowy power swirling around the room.

His other hand was upturned and directed at the Halopod, drawing extra power from it as it moved closer to Megan in her defence. The Halopod had nearly quadrupled in size as it exerted its power. A translucent ethereal blanket of protection ballooned out and covered Megan.

She crouched down in fear, as the magic sought to grasp hold of her. Tendrils, like cold ghostly fingers, touched her arms and legs. She could feel herself being disassembled. Her very cells felt like they were being stretched apart by some unknown force. She tried to cry out in terror, but her voice would not work. Her words were muted and still born. Nothing came out of her mouth. She could only think that surely she would be saved. Sagent Nah was here and Gemma as well. Her thoughts became unnaturally elongated and felt disjointed and muddled. She was being taken apart at the very smallest fragments of her being. Was this it for her? Was this death she was experiencing? She saw herself as a long stream of particles and specks travelling along a sort of cosmic path. She was still aware and that scared her all the more. She could actually see it happening. Then there was nothing. All went black.

Sagent Nah looked on in disbelief as Megan began to disappear. He felt that his power was ineffective. Nothing was working. Even with the combined power of the Halopod, the course of action could not be stopped. She was being disassembled.

Gemma wailed in grief and frustration, changing shape into a small teardrop, and falling back into the locket. The two halves closed, before it too disappeared.

The white Zaurlock slumped down in defeat as Megan's image diminished and faded completely from his sight. He had lost the battle. The light of his power also evaporated in his disillusionment.

* * *

Draig sat on his oversized throne and waited. He knew exactly what the outcome would be from his iniquitous conjure. The plan would unfold just as he desired. Megan would be disassembled and brought to him here on Mount Isnar, where he would then finish his empirical work without interference.

Did Sagent Nah really think his rudimentary deflection shield would stop him? It was so easy for him to break through it. Yes, he was indeed becoming more powerful each day. Was there no end to his capabilities? He would rule the Eastlands realm, and Henrik would bow to him.

Soon and very soon Megan would arrive, and he would hold the key to King Henrik's heart and soul. He would do anything to save his beloved daughter.

As he mused on these things, a shimmer of light particles began to take shape in front of him.

"Ah, look who is coming," he said aloud speaking to no one in particular. His HuverWort screeched a gurgled response.

The outline of a crouching person slowly formed. The silhouette gradually became more solid increasing in depth and clarity.

Megan opened her eyes and looked straight at Draig.

She did not speak but averted her eyes, continuing to look around the room, and trying to establish just where she was.

Still seated, he stared back at her. The intensity of his sharp inky eyes was not softened by the snakeskin mask he wore over them. His face contorted, into what appeared to be an amused expression. Two fingers and a thumb stroked his shaggy bearded chin as he waited for her to speak.

"I know who you are." Megan stood awkwardly to her full height, squaring her shoulders in mock defiance. Inwardly she was terrified. It was obvious that she was alone and without help. She told herself to be brave and not to show fear. It took all her self control not to break down and weep. Her insides churned with the realization of her predicament and panic welled just below the façade of courage. Her breath came in short gasps. She tried to slow it down and remain calm, but her heart pumped even faster.

"I'm sure you do my pretty one," the twisted smirk broke into a full smile showing clearly the gap in the set of crooked and yellowed upper teeth, where the one tooth was missing. For all his magical skills he had not yet managed to create a new tooth for himself. Not that self image mattered particularly to him. Vengeance was much more important, and he now had the little princess fully in his control.

"You will not get away with this Draig." Megan surprised herself with her own air of confidence and bravado.

"Really, I thought that I already had, you are here are you not?" He smugly replied while he absently scratched his ear.

"What do you want of me? I have done nothing to you." She noticed as she spoke, that her voice sounded somehow deeper than she thought it should sound. It was more mature, and stronger, than her voice had been before. Before what, she did not know. She still felt a little addled in her mind. She hoped that the feeling would soon go, as it was very uncomfortable.

"You speak the truth young Megan. However, what I have planned for you will remain my secret. You will find out soon enough."

Standing to his feet, he continued, "You are free to roam around my fortress home, however, do not try to escape, or I may not be as nice to you, as I am right now." He turned away and then looked back.

"And by the way, do not think that your wispy little friend will aid you this time, I have put a seal on your locket, which cannot be undone."

Megan self consciously touched the necklace containing her little messenger.

He eyed her intensely, making her feel very conspicuous. "Your first epiphany is about to happen. I hope you enjoy it, I know I will."

His sinister and threatening tone quieted Megan. She felt suddenly unsure of herself, and sat down on the hard floor, turning away from Draig's penetrating gaze.

She could only imagine what he had in store for her. It could not be that bad she hoped. She consoled herself, thinking that last time he had morphed her into a fox; it had only lasted one day. She had been able to change back without any real damage done, although, he did try to burn her alive. That thought sparked a whole new set of dire possibilities raging through her mind. He obviously did not need a valid reason, to persecute her, or even to harm her. Her position as princess in the kingdom did not seem to afford her, the protection it deserved.

She was certain Sagent Nah would be doing his best to rescue her. Believing that gave her some comfort, but at the same time, she wondered if he had the power to overcome Draig. So far, it appeared to be all Draig's way. Her father would be worried, and would dedicate all his vast resources to finding her, and in bringing Draig to justice, but he was limited to the physical realm. Draig's advantage was in the realm of the supernatural. It had to be Sagent Nah who would challenge his power and dominion, and bring him to heel. He had not succeeded thus far.

Megan almost lost heart when she considered this. Where did her hope lie? Her youth gave her ideals regarding the force for good, and how it would always prevail. She found it hard to believe, that someone would do evil just because they could, without considering the innocent. Surely Draig would see reason. What did he hope to gain by abducting her? Should she try to seek out, what it was, he wanted. Her father could surely grant him almost anything within reason, but he seemed bent on just being in total control.

"You seem very deep in thought, young princess."

She chose to ignore him, and did not turn around or acknowledge him in any way. The main reason being, that she did not know as yet, how she would manage to convince him to abandon his actions, and return her safely to her father. She recalled his attitude last time she had tried to offer him a reward for helping her. He placed little value on anything her father could give him. He was more interested in some ill conceived notion, that her father had irretrievably wronged him. It was obviously some sort of retaliation.

It suddenly dawned on her, that she had been thinking thoughts, which were not those of a ten year old. They seemed to be thoughts, and rationales, of someone much older.

How could that be? Did something happen, when Draig disassembled, and then reassembled her? She looked around the room for a mirror.

"There is one to your left."

Draig had been reading her thoughts. She had no idea how she could prevent this from happening.

"Don't you want to see you new self? Well, maybe not so new, perhaps older self," he roared with laughter, which deteriorated into a minor coughing fit. The echoes of his mirth resounded off the cave walls, as he stood, and rotated the mirror around to face her.

She looked at the image in the glass before her. She was beautiful. It certainly looked like her, but she was older, perhaps eighteen or nineteen years of age. A deluge of mixed feelings flooded into her mind. On one hand, she was appalled that she had been changed and was no longer a ten year old, and yet, there was a real sense of excitement welling up inside her, as she looked at the stunning beauty of the person in the mirror.

"Well Megan, do you like your new self?" Draig came around to stand admiringly behind her.

She did not know how to respond. She was dumbfounded.

"Now, you can begin to appreciate my power. I can grant you life's years, and I can take them away." He was enjoying this.

But his words fell on deaf ears, as the questions and doubts raced unfettered through her mind. Was this really happening? Had she lost forever eight or more years of her life? Could she ever regain them, or were they eternally inaccessible to her as a mere mortal. Her head was spinning with the weight of the revelation.

She made an immense effort to calm herself, and to settle her raging thoughts. Look to the positives in the situation, her father had told her so many times. She would anchor her sanity on that thinking. So she was older. Surely that meant that her thinking was more mature, that she could conduct herself as an adult, and not as a child.

"A wise idea." Draig's voice interrupted her reasoning.

Megan became angry. Draig was harvesting her private thoughts. She felt violated. How could she stop him? Like a penny dropping the idea dawned on her. Immediately, she divided off an area of her mind, to be dedicated to her own private thoughts only. She then continued her thoughts, knowing that they would now exclude Draig's access.

Sagent Nah had taught her to detach and separate parts of her mind. She was now free to think, without having his unwanted audience. The white Zaurlock had insisted that she be schooled and drilled in this practice. Did he foresee this day coming, or, was he just being thorough in his training and education of a royal princess. It did not matter. What mattered was that she could do it. She could keep private the thoughts, that she did not want Draig to know about. Conversely, she could plant her ideas in his mind, by allowing him to overhear only selected thoughts. This was good. She had clawed back some control in the situation.

Chapter 6

Sagent Nah stood before King Henrik. His head was bowed shamefully. He dare not look directly into the king's eyes.

"Forgive me Lord … I tried my best using all my powers to prevent this from happening, but Draig's magical supremacy has increased to such an extent, that I could not stop him." Keeping his eyes averted, Nah continued. "It seems, my lord that Draig is drawing his power from sources, other than those permitted by our statutes of enchantment laid down by the Council of Rah judiciary."

King Henrik's mouth was set in a grimace. If he had heard Nah, he did not show it. His brow knitted in consternation. Internal thoughts and recriminations dominated and plagued his mind. His face reflected an uncustomary weary pallor. Nothing was ever too much for this capable monarch to bear; he could always provide adequate, if not on most occasions, excellent solutions to any problem. This particular situation, involved his only child who he cherished with a fierce paternal, and uncompromising love. His only daughter had been abducted, and he did not know exactly why it had happened, or where she was being held. He felt emasculated and powerless. He was king and sovereign ruler, but it did not help that he could raise an army of one thousand battle hardened soldiers, who would lay down their lives at his command. He had placed his hope, in the white Zaurlock's expertise and experience in the supernatural world to ensure his daughters safety. He had failed. His first inclination was to lash out and inflict his frustration and wrath on Nah. But he realized that this would produce no worthwhile outcome. He needed the white Zaurlock's help, and alienating him through unfair treatment would not rectify the situation.

These thoughts tore at his reasoning abilities as he sat despondently on his throne. The full court was assembled. They all waited attentively for his next directive. He was not just a figurehead, but he was a soldier king. In numerous arenas of war he had fought bravely alongside his men in battle, and they and the general populace respected him immensely. He was crowned monarch at a relatively young age, and had to take on the responsibilities of governing the new kingdom as an adolescent. His father was killed fighting in the Battle of Lords for the sovereignty of the realm. Over the years, he had grown and matured into the role, and even though he was soon to turn just forty-five years old, he was seen by all, as an even-handed and fair ruler. Why had the gods chosen to reprove him in this way?

All were silent, as he rose to his feet, and walked to the edge of the dais. "I make this solemn and irrevocable edict this day. Draig, the black Zaurlock has committed treason, by abducting a member of the royal family. He is henceforth banished from my kingdom, and if he chooses to remain within the kingdom's bounds, he will be hunted down, seized, and brought to my court to be dealt with by the Table of Wisdom elders, using the full extent and power of kingdom law."

He paused to allow his words to take effect before continuing.

"Sagent Nah, Chief Court Zaurlock and advisor to the king, I charge you to go forth to the Council of Rah, and seek out whatever power or means are necessary to rescue my daughter, and to overcome and defeat the treasonous abductor Draig. Do not return, unless you have fulfilled this charge. You will leave on your assignment this day, without further delay."

Sagent Nah bowed in respect and withdrew immediately to prepare to leave for the holy city of Alabasteil, where the Council of Rah deliberated on all things enchanted, and where young Zaurlocks were trained for service within the kingdom. He could not transport himself there instantly by magic, as this particular function was tied only to Megan's Halopod, and could not be used at random. He would have to make the journey physically, which he knew would take precious time he did not have to spare.

Sagent Nah had completed his training in Alabasteil around one hundred and fifty years ago. He had returned to the charmed city on an annual pilgrimage each year since. In one way he was delighted that he was going back there. It was always a time of refreshment and revitalization. Each time he visited the seat of magic, he could feel his powers altering, and becoming more cohesive, and pragmatic. This however, was not a recreational pursuit. The charge that had been placed upon him by his liege was onerous, and heavy with responsibility. Princess Megan's life was at stake, and probably his own, if he failed in his mission.

* * *

Try as she might, Megan could not stop looking at her image in the mirror. Draig had bought her a chair, sarcastically portraying himself as a gentleman waiting on a lady. She had ignored his contemptuous attitude, as she thought that this was the best response. She did not even acknowledge the fine clothing he had provided for her. The image of a seated young lady reflected back at her. Is this what she would really look like had she matured naturally, or was she some disdainful fabrication orchestrated by Draig, as part of his reprehensible plan? She liked to think that she would have turned out this way. She was beautiful. Not a blemish marred her perfect skin and features; her hair was thick, and had a natural gentle wave, as it sat shoulder length. It shone a golden blonde, with streaks the colour of flaxen, accentuating the waves. Her eyes were the feature that most convinced her, that this was indeed how she would have grown, they were unmistakably hers.

She was aware of Draig's intense presence, and had purposefully allowed him to listen in on her thoughts. This would alleviate any suspicion he may have, that she had the ability to cordon off her most private thoughts from him. Small consolation, what could she do anyway to make good her escape, or send for aid. He had sealed her locket, and nobody knew where they were. She was certain that he would have spelled the cavern, so that it could not be located easily.

Her thoughts were interrupted by Draig's raspy voice feigning sympathy. "I am afraid your time has come my pretty. I only made you like this to show you what you will be missing out on. What a pity, so beautiful."

"What do you mean?" Megan's bravado belied the dread which welled up inside her. She felt the coppery taste of bile in her mouth. A sense of impending danger dogged her mind.

"I do not answer your questions," he yelled fiercely at her, and spat as he spoke.

The unexpected flare up of his rage astounded her. Was he insane? Surely she had a right to ask what he meant without him flying into a fit of rage. She thought that she was right, he probably was insane.

As quickly as it rose, his anger abated. He continued with his sickly sweet tone. "Tell me princess, did you enjoy your time as a fox?"

Megan would never admit to him that she had in fact enjoyed certain aspects of the experience. She drew the curtain within her mind, and continued her reverie in the confines of her private inner world. Being a fox had offered her a departure from the ordinary. After all, how many people have actually been a fox for a day during their lifetime? As a fox, she had experienced a heightened awareness of her senses. She could identify and distinguish between things by smell, and her hearing and eyesight were extraordinary. She could run, and perform acts of agility which she never dreamed she could accomplish. As a human, she had always been rather awkward when it came to physical feats.

Draig stood to his full imposing height and stepped closer to her. His face had lost all semblance of the previous pretence of sympathy, and glowered with an intense malevolence. "Your father is responsible for your demise. He was the one who rejected me, and now I will wreak my vengeance on you, his daughter."

She hated what she had just heard. The unfairness of it offended her sensibilities to the extreme. He was obviously delusional in the way he viewed the situation. Anger welled up inside her, but she was powerless against him. Even in the physical sense she was hopelessly inept. He stood over seven feet tall, and she could see the robustness of his muscular frame even through the loose fitting robes. He flaunted his psychological advantage mercilessly. He was a man. She was just a girl. He was over three hundred years of age and she was … well ten, or perhaps eighteen. Then there was the magic. He had proven that he was the most powerful Zaurlock in the Eastlands realm. Panic threatened to overwhelm her. She allowed him to sense her fear. Maybe in some way it might appease his unbalanced need, and persuade him to show mercy.

He smiled.

The fear he sensed actually fuelled his desires. He liked his victims to be afraid. It empowered him like nothing else did. A low moan of satisfaction came from deep in his throat.

Now the terror rose unabated within her. She had worsened the situation, if that were possible. She could not prevent the look of fear from showing on her face. Tears flowed unchecked down her cheeks. She wanted her father. She yearned for the safety of his strong arms around her, protecting her. That was not going to happen. She was alone and vulnerable. Deep in the recesses of her heart she knew that she had to make a stand. Dredging the depths of her soul, she sought strength. She was the king's daughter. Her heritage was that of a long line of brave and courageous fighters. A lineage steeped in power which had conquered nations, and ruled kingdoms. Now she could feel the innate strength building up within her being. Strength, stemming from centuries of ancestral crusades for good was drawing together, deep in her psyche. Fear dissipated as the strength welled up from her very essence.

Standing to her feet, she squarely faced up to Draig. Looking up into his face, she noticed that her action had produced the slightest glimmer of doubt reflected in the eyes, which were partially obscured behind the snakeskin mask. Could it possibly be that she possessed more power for good than she knew. Was his resolve waning? The intensity of his gaze phased in and out. The windows of his soul revealed a shift in his mental presence from reality, to somewhere on the fringes of insanity, and back again.

With her confidence on the rise, she now courted the idea, that she could regain her freedom and exercise some sort of control in the situation. Taking advantage of his momentary lack of focus, she started to move sideways and away from him.

His reaction was swift and cruel. He raised his hands, and with two pointed fingers dealt out the punishment mercilessly.

The dual shafts of searing pain struck the middle of her back like two fangs of some massive snake. She had never felt such torturous pain before. Its paralysing force dropped her to her knees. She collapsed forward, and lay prone with her teeth tightly clenched, bearing up under the rawness of the pain. She tried to scream, but no sound came forth.

Thankfully the pain ceased suddenly. It felt like the venomous fangs had been withdrawn, but she still could not move a muscle.

"Do not ever attempt that again." The menacing voice was delivered with such ferocity, it caused Megan's body to flinch involuntarily. "Enough of the games."

Raising his hands and speaking forth a shouted invocation, he turned to the face the rear wall of the cavern.

In the centre of the disproportionately high wall, a huge etching of an eagle landing dominated the multi dimensioned, layered terracotta surface. Its fiery red eyes the epitome of evil. At his command, two huge doors creaked open, splitting the image of the eagle in half as they parted. Out of the dark recess behind emerged a large gilded cage. Shaped like ancient temple with a curved roof structure, it shone brightly with a golden patina emitting magical power. It moved under its own influence out of the recess, and into the middle of the room. It was high enough for a man to stand erect when inside. Suspended well above the height of Draig's throne, it sat poised in the air without any ropes or wires supporting it.

Draig waved his hand in a downward motion. The cage lowered to the floor. With another command he opened the golden door wide. Turning to the still form on the floor he said, "Your new home is ready my princess."

She lay on the floor trapped in her rigid body, unable to turn her head around to see what Draig was talking about. This was much worse than she had imagined.

Chapter 7

Quan the Gimp sat astride his small grey donkey. The animal was his preferred mount. It made him appear unobtrusive and foolish, belying his potent ability to aggressively attack and defend his charge when confronted with danger. He was fully prepared and ready to make the journey to Alabasteil. The saddle bags were packed to overflowing with provisions, and he was equipped for every unseen circumstance likely to occur. He always prided himself on his forethought and rigorous preparation. A weather proof cape made of tanned sheep skin donned his shoulders and draped back over the rump of the donkey. He wore no hat, as he preferred to feel the sun on the thickened skin of his oversized hairless head. He had a large protruding forehead denoting his acute intelligence. Pointed ears, with ungroomed hair in the elongated holes, stuck out at almost right angles to his head. His eyes were big and round, with irises so dark, that the pupils were indistinguishable. They dominated his roughly oval shaped countenance, more so than his flattened nose, which had been broken more than once. The years had weathered his face so that he looked every bit of his one hundred and twenty years. Deep furrows creased his brow, and his eyebrow hair grew vertically to halfway up his forehead. This was a distinctive feature of his unusual race. The vestige of a long time healed, but grisly scar snaked its way down his right cheek to his deeply cleft chin. A small bow and quiver of arrows was slung across his back. A curved dagger sat unobtrusively in the belt of his chamois leather britches. He was tall for a Gimp, which was really not very tall at all. He only came up to Sagent Nah's belt buckle when standing his full height in his heeled boots. His heavily muscled and hairless torso with his distinctive yellowish skin always made him stand out in a crowd.

Sagent Nah was almost set to leave. His warhorse, a strong grey stallion scraped the ground with its hoof and snorted plumes of hot breath from its nostrils into the crisp morning air. Nah stroked its thick neck. He was also keen to be started. He looked over to his friend Quan and felt a sense of gratitude that he had so willingly set aside his own interests to come with him on this crucial assignment.

He had especially gone to his old friend Quan to ask him to accompany him on his journey to Alabasteil. Quan was not to be underestimated when it came to his innate ability to sense danger, and his incredible ferocity in battle. He was unconditionally loyal, and would defend his friends to the end. He had proven himself many times before. Supernatural powers and abilities flowed unchecked from Quan once his battle ire flared. This mission was far too important for it to be thwarted for any reason. Quan was there to ensure that the white Zaurlock reached his destination and returned safely.

Nah's mind was filled with trepidation as he made his final preparations. The journey to Alabasteil would take nearly two weeks to complete, and then there was the return journey to consider. Did he have the luxury of time? He had sent a spectrum scan across the ether seeking Megan's whereabouts, but it produced nothing. Draig was obviously blocking his attempts. He hoped with all his heart that his brother was still just being obstructive, and did not have a more sinister agenda in mind concerning the princess. Nah had difficulty understanding why Draig was so set on revenge. The supposed cause did not justify his radical course of action. It pointed to something else; something far more frightening and fearsome. The increase in his power of late was indeed suspect. In the last thirty years, his power had increased by degrees, but this latest spike was a tenfold increase in just a single year. Had he gone completely to the other side, and was drawing upon the evil one himself? Nah hoped that he had not compromised his integrity for the sake of gaining greater power. His brother had always been ambitious and ruthless in his quest for power, but he had never in furthering his cause resorted to abduction and possibly worse. Nah held strong in his belief that in the end, good would prevail, and he would find a solution. There must be a greater and more profound a reason for all this. Megan was an innocent piece of the puzzle. He fretted over the possibility of failure. Not so much because of what the king would do to him, but more out of his genuine concern for the princess's welfare. He held a deep affection and devotion for Megan. It tore at his heart to contemplate that anything would happen to her while under his watch. Putting aside the worrisome thoughts, he turned his mind to the task ahead. Steeling himself against more fearful imaginations, he resolved to put all his effort into succeeding in the task set before him.

As the first crimson streaks of the new dawn illuminated the sky, the Zaurlock mounted his steed and headed off down the cobbled track leading away from the Keep. Quan followed close behind him.

* * *

Megan could not move. Time seemed to lose all relevance. How long she had lain there, she could not fathom. She blinked back the tears which came involuntarily. She felt helpless and abandoned. He was in total control. She no longer asked herself why he was doing this. There was no sane reason or justification for his actions. What mattered was keeping her own mind calm and determined to achieve a positive outcome. She told herself that she was strong, and brave, and that she would prevail in the end if she just kept going and did not give up. The paralysis was concerning. Was it permanent? She tried once more to move her hand. Nothing happened.

The floor suddenly seemed to move beneath her. She felt herself being lifted into the air by some force completely apart from her. Her unresponsive body still in crouched position was moved through the air toward her gilded jail.

With his hands extended, Draig directed her travel with magic, sneering and looking down his nose at her as she passed by him and through the cage door. The door clanged loudly closed behind her as she was lowered to the cage floor. Pain wreaked her inert body, but she could not move to relieve the cramping muscles. Her face pressed down on the hard floor. She felt the dribble run unchecked down her chin. She felt miserable.

The sound of an enchantment rang through the air sealing her prison door with a spell. The release that came after that was euphoric. She felt as if life was returning to her lifeless body. She could move again. She stretched out her bunched and knotted muscles, revelling in the freedom of movement.

When she was able, she stood unsteadily. Draig was still in the room, but with his back toward her.

Frustration overcame her. She flung herself at the bars of the cage yelling at him. "Let me out you madman. You have no right to hold me here. I am Princess Megan, and you will pay dearly for what you are doing."

Draig languidly turned to face her. He did not reply, but just looked disparagingly at her. He chose to ignore her recriminations and returned to what he was doing previously.

He was studying some sort of spell book. His head lowered in concentration and his back toward her. Megan heard his feint murmurings as he moved his arms in set rhythmic patterns. His voice at times becoming high pitched, and raucous, and then falling away to no more than a mutter. It seemed like an eternity before he ceased his conjuring.

When he faced her again his face was almost serene. He had removed the snakeskin mask which exposed even more the intensity of his black eyes. Moving closer to the bars of her cage, he again smiled his greasy smile. Megan shuddered at the prospects which lay before her. She withdrew to the back of the cage, putting herself as far away from him as she could.

"You will change the way you think about me Megan." She heard his breath coming in short gasps. "Now begins your trial."

She flinched, as she felt the first wave of diabolism flow over her. A scream escaped from her lips through her gritted teeth. The second wave quickly followed, and then a succession of invasive tremors shook her body to the core. The level of pain increased with each undulating wave of his spell.

It finished abruptly. She fell, exhausted face down on the floor of the cage from the intensity of her brief, but painful ordeal. Her chest rose and fell with each heaving breath. Her hair was bedraggled and lathered in sweat. The effect of the spell depleted her of strength, and she slipped into a welcome lack of consciousness.

* * *

In a semi aware state, Megan thought she could smell something raw and fleshy. She fought her way up through the heaviness of her spell induced sleep and into half wakefulness. Her body ached with the tension and discomfort of being in one position for too long. She did not know how much time had passed. It could have been one turning of the hourglass, or much longer, she had no idea. Her last memory was of Draig as he meted out his spell upon her. She winced at the thought of the horrific pain he had so casually dealt out. She noticed the rays of sunlight coming through the irregular hole in the cave wall. It must have been some sort of airway providing fresh air to the dingy interior. It gave her the impression that she may have been underground. Her logical mind reasoned that it must be morning, just which morning she could not know. As her eyes opened slightly and became more accustomed to the light, she saw a plate of raw meat directly in front of her on the floor. She sat up with a start suddenly realizing where she was. Her head ached, and her vision was blurred, but she could definitely identify the rancid smell of raw meat. What possible use could she have for that?

"Allow me to explain."

She looked around seeking the source of the voice. Now the memories came flooding back. She was Draig's prisoner. He had abducted her, and cast some iniquitous spell over her, saying something about her trial was now beginning.

Draig observed Megan closely. Like a bird in a cage she was trapped. He and he alone determined what happened to her next. She would come to love him eventually. It would take time. The morphing process would change her thinking. He questioned himself as to how his greatest magical feat was progressing? It was only the first day and the signs were beginning to show. He breathed in a long breath, sighing in the satisfaction of witnessing her morphing first hand. This was different to the immature effort which had morphed her the first time into a fox. That experiment had proven mildly amusing, but was nothing compared to this. It was but a foretaste of greater things to come. Not a serious endorsement of his prowess as an alphawizard.

Would her resistance prove vexing? She must in the end come to realize that there is no escape, and, that she must obey and worship him as lord and master. Would he have to resort to using the Searing Twitch to convince her to think in this way?

The Searing Twitch was his latest weapon used to persuade reluctant lessers to do his will. He had successfully trained his HuverWort to render it completely obedient and malleable, when it had been hopelessly rebellious and headstrong. The Searing Twitch was a short rod like device magically charged, which when applied to the skin released a searing band of pain to the recipient, usually ending in unconsciousness. He hoped that he did not have to resort to this form of persuasion with the Princess. Not that he held any real reservations about using it on her. He did not have time or patience to pander to anyone who would not comply with his wishes to the letter.

"The raw meat is for you to eat. You may not like it immediately, but soon you will relish it."

"I will not eat raw meat. I will starve before I do," Megan retorted steadfastly as she eyed the bloody mound on the plate before her.

"Very well, we shall see how you view it in a short while. Oh yes, and would you like to see how things may be changing for you."

He again waved his hand in an upward motion chanting a short invocation.

The bars of her cage began to merge with other bars, dividing themselves into segments all around her. Each segment changed into a mirror turning on its own axis. The entire cage also began to rotate in what felt like the opposite direction to the mirrors. She experienced a sense of giddiness as all of the mirrors rotated independently of the other. She closed her eyes to stop the feeling from overwhelming her completely. When finally the turning stopped, she waited for her internal balance to return before opening her eyes again. From one of the mirror segments she viewed her image. It did not look exactly like her. Her features were not as fine as the beautiful girl she had seen before. Something had altered shape. She looked slightly feline in her appearance. Her cheek bones were positioned higher, and there were fine black hairs growing over her entire face.

She quickly checked her body. The same fine hair was evident on her arms and legs.

"Enough for today."

With a word from Draig, the mirrors disappeared and the bars returned to their previous form. Draig marvelled at his abilities. This was not just a temporary morphing lasting one day. Megan had been able to quite easily undo the vulpine fox morph with a little help from her friends. This time he would be much more thorough. It will take a greater period to perform, but would be much harder to unravel, and would last much longer.

"Please do not do this to me. Let me go, and I will speak to my father for you. Tell me what it is that you want, and I will get it for you …" Megan's voice trailed off in desperation as she saw the pleasure that her pleading was giving her captor.

She tried reasoning with him.

"Perhaps you were wronged by my father for not making you Chief Zaurlock, but that does not warrant this degree of retribution. You have lived for centuries, and surely you have learned that life is not always fair …"

"Indeed it isn't," Draig cut off her sharply, "You should save your platitudes for those of a more feeble nature who may be persuaded to listen to you. I have made up my mind, and, you will not avert the course that I have set for you. Each day, you will experience a greater degree of change, until you are completely morphed into the animal form of a black panther. I understand your father likes black panthers."

Megan's brow knitted in consternation. A black panther? Why a black panther? Her only consolation was that this was not her first experience in being morphed into animal form. She had survived the last time, and she would survive this time. Draig would only win if she capitulated and allowed him to win. Her father had taught her to be strong, and she would not let him down. She had to admit though, that she was frightened by the changes to her physical self that she saw in the mirror. She had not experienced a slow morphing before. The last time she had awoken already changed. Whatever faced her in the coming days, she was determined to endure it, with as much dignity, as she could rally.

Chapter 8

Quan had collected enough firewood in his short stocky arms to make their camp fire. They had travelled for the best part of all the daylight hours, and had made good time. Quan's donkey had shown surprising tenacity, speed, and endurance, in keeping pace with Nah's warhorse throughout the long day. It indicated strongly, that perhaps some supernatural ability, had been instilled into the beast by Quan himself.

They sat facing each other, watching in silence the flames licking around the burning logs, as their evening meal of spice soup was warming.

Talk had been brief as they travelled. They had concentrated on gaining as much distance as they could through the daylight hours, but now they were free to speak about the reason for the journey, and the obvious haste.

"My brother has changed Quan. He is no longer keeping within the bounds of enchantment law. By abducting Princess Megan, he has also breached the most obvious kingdom law."

Quan's intelligent eyes watched his old friend, as he spoke the words with obvious grief. The Gimp shared his friend's concern. A Zaurlock of Draig's standing in the kingdom, breaking tradition, and the law, in this most serious way spoke of a rift in the very fabric of society that had survived intact for centuries, by abiding by the statutes.

"I feel especially responsible as I am the Chief Court Zaurlock, and Draig is my brother." Emotion welled up in him as he spoke. "I fear that he is insane, and I am filled with trepidation for the safety of the Princess."

"They are certainly not the actions of a sane being." Even though Gimps were not renowned for their sympathetic ear, Quan tried to console his friend. "You have your heart in the right place, Nah. I have known you a long time, and from what I can see, you always try to do your best. What you are dealing with is a rebel, and an outlaw, who has broken away from all, that is reasonable and right. I fear that he himself does not realize that he is being used by the malevolent one for his unsavoury purpose in the earth. Missing out on a position does not justify abduction. It is insane behaviour at its worst."

With an affirming nod of his head, Nah replied, "It certainly appears that way. I would have thought that Draig would resist any involvement with the malevolent one. His training and experience spanning over one hundred years should have given him the wisdom, and the caution, not to get involved. The only way he could be involved, is if he has willingly sought to engage the dark side. I suppose, he could have reached the pinnacle of his abilities. He has sought all that was available to him in this earthly realm through devastative magic and perhaps, he still did not feel fulfilled."

The Gimp was not one to continue surmising.

"What can we do about it?" he asked emphatically.

"The king has decreed that I visit the holy city of Alabasteil, and seek a solution from the Council elders there. I am not certain, that even they, with their great power and control of all things enchanted, can easily resolve this." Nah's reply was cut short by two things occurring simultaneously.

Quan's face had taken on a distant and mystical expression, and a rock, lying on the ground beside them began to radiate evidence of a magical presence.

The Gimp's eyes seemed focused on something far in the distance. He was irresponsive to Nah's voice trying to bring him back to reality, and the present.

Sagent Nah immediately engaged his ether vision, to seek out the source of the alchemy emanating from the rock. He reasoned that, as the two events had occurred at the same time that the two were related and, that whatever was in the rock was what was affecting Quan. His ether vision rays pierced the rock surface producing a gurgled screech. The HuverWort abruptly changed its appearance from the rock, into its single winged actual form. It sped off rapidly flying just above the ground, raising the dust as it went. It crested a small hillock, and disappeared from site.

Nah turned his attention to Quan; he had never seen his strong companion in such a comatose state. The Gimp sat motionless, and continued to stare into nothingness with unblinking eyes. His brows were knitted in concentration. He had been seated on the ground, but now, he was suspended, and hovered about waist high above the forest floor. His arms moved into a folded position, with his legs crossed over each other. An aura like shimmer surrounded him like an oversized halo. He watched in wonder. Quan's mouth began to speak, but it was not the voice of the Gimp. It had a mystical resonance which Nah had never heard before.

"Through the mouth of my servant Quan, I speak truth."

The voice paused before continuing.

"This is the prophecy that I the holy one speak this day. The shroud between earth and deep earth has been rent. Evil has pervaded the earth through one who seeks it wrongly. It brings with it persecution of my innocent, who I have now chosen as the vessel to right the wrong. Seek out the Stone of Deliverance, for it belongs with my innocent. In her hand, it shall cause the shroud to be restored, and evil to once again be contained. Seek and find the Stone in the holy city."

Sagent Nah was almost overwhelmed with the power of the presence. He struggled to remain standing on his feet, and fell face down in reverential awe.

He did not know how much time had passed. He had slipped into some sort of trancelike state where time had no meaning. He raised his head and opened his eyes. Looking around, he noticed that the fire had burned out. It looked like it had been out for some time. Quan was lying on the ground a short distance from him. He appeared to be in a deep sleep. The first rays of the new dawn were just appearing over the horizon. It was morning.

He stood and briefly stretched his aching muscles. Moving over to where Quan lay, he leant over and touched the Gimp's arm. The reaction was immediate. In a flash Quan had pulled his dagger, and placed it at Nah's throat.

"Wait," was all Nah could think to say.

Quan smiled and said in good humour, "How many times

have I told you not to sneak up on me like that? It is dangerous."

The smile quickly left his lips when he noticed the dour look on the white Zaurlock's face.

Walking away and back to the burnt out campfire, Nah turned and said. "We need to speak."

* * *

Megan seemed now to understand the pattern. Each day, she was, by degrees being morphed from her human self into the animal form of a black panther. To what end she had no idea. What she could do to stop it? … She had even less inspiration to offer herself. She knew that the process was progressing because the raw meat, which she had rejected outright on the first day, now seemed more appealing. Perhaps it was just her growing hunger. She felt she had not eaten in days. The increase in black hair appearing on her body was becoming more evident.

Rasita's words about the prophecy dropped suddenly and uninvited into her mind.

"the renting of the shroud between earth and deep earth"

Was there a greater purpose in her persecution?

"a chosen one who would be persecuted without cause"

It would certainly make this trial more bearable for her, if she thought that she was fulfilling some preordained destiny which was of earth-shattering importance to all of humanity.

"would be the one to right the wrong"

What power did she have against the work of evil being perpetrated? She had not even been able to restrain Draig in the slightest thus far.

The words of the prophecy did not inspire her particularly. She had no way of knowing if, in fact she was really the chosen one.

Her thoughts returned sharply to the starkness of her present reality. She was trapped, and being transformed into a beast by an insane evil Zaurlock and she was powerless to stop him.

She tried to collect her thoughts which were becoming more confused as time went on.

On the second day, which she thought was yesterday; Draig had left her the entire time by herself, and only came to her after the last rays of sunlight faded from the air shaft in the cave wall.

The changes in sun's rays coming through the opening were her only gauge of time.

He had cast another spell on her which seemed less painful, but left her unconscious once more. She had not awoken again, until what she could only imagine was the morning of the third day.

She had been awake only a short time, when Draig emerged from somewhere within the recesses of the cave.

Not choosing to speak to her, he immediately began the ritual of the mirrors once again. He seemed derive some pleasure from watching how she reacted each time her image was freshly displayed to her. This time was no exception. Megan let out an uncontrolled gasp at the grotesque image appearing in the mirror. She had changed dramatically in the time which passed since she had first seen herself as a beautiful eighteen year old. Her cheek bones were much higher now, and her ears were more cup shaped, and they had moved more to the top of her head. Her eyes were much sharper, and were turning green with the pupils changing to an almost vertical position and form. The misshapen feline face was nearly fully covered in short black fur. She had already noticed with dismay, that her hands and feet were more like those of an animal now, with long claws where her finger and toenails had once been. Her acceptance of her lot as perhaps being part of her destiny just a short time ago quickly evaporated with the shock of the realization which now invaded her psyche. She wept openly and convulsed with racking sobs. The mirrors reverted back to bars again with a clang, reminding her of the reality of her entrapment.

Draig appeared impassive to her reaction of shock and horror. He pursed his lips, as if contemplating his next action. He went over to a small bench in the corner of the room. Opening a drawer, he produced a short rod like shaft. As his hand made contact with the handle, the rod crackled with power, emitting bursts of sharp lightning like tendrils. He winced slightly at the pain, which the device was also giving him as he contacted it. He had obviously become inured to the razor-sharp pain sensation coming from the Searing Twitch; otherwise he would not be able to use it effectively on others.

"I would like to ask you a question Megan." Draig walked from the bench to the bars of her floating prison. "Are you ready to obey me implicitly, and to call me lord?"

She eyed the rod he held threateningly in his hand. Immediately she drew the curtain across in her mind, keeping safe and separated the one area that no one would touch, ever. She silently thanked Sagent Nah for teaching her how to do this. Draig may turn her to his will, but she would always retain this part of her being. She would not allow him access, no matter what horrible things he did.

She was the chosen one who had been given great responsibility to outwork the prophecy. She chose to believe this. She needed a cause to cling to as she sensed with foreboding, the imminent threat.

She was unprepared for the shooting pain she felt, as he touched her leg with the Searing Twitch. Her scream wailed out unchecked from deep in her throat. It sounded more like the howl of a wild animal. Instinctively, she lashed out at him with her clawed paw, only the bars preventing her now sharp claws from raking this face. He drew back in fear not expecting her to be the aggressor yet.

He retaliated with another touch of the Twitch. Megan screamed again, recoiling, but standing to challenge him at the same time. Her mouth opened, baring the half grown fangs in an ugly snarl.

At some point, she had switched to communicating in the speech of the wild feline predator she was becoming.

"You will never control me," she heard herself saying, "I would sooner die than be reduced to being your servant."

"We shall see," he responded in an understandable language that was clearly not Eastlander tongue. "Perhaps another day will prove you wrong. Enjoy your meat."

He was about to depart when his HuverWort entered the room screeching and gurgling as it came.

Draig raised a hand and stopped it in mid flight. It noticed immediately the Searing Twitch still in Draig's hand, and it flinched, and drew back in terror, its fleshy eyelids moving nervously up and down over the bug like eyes.

"Do not fear my little minion. I will not use it again on you."

The HuverWort continued to eye the rod fearfully, but did not move from its position, hovering motionless in the air.

"What news do you bring me?" Draig's voice took on a smooth dulcet tone in an attempt to calm his nervous underling messenger.

"A prophecy has been proclaimed. A prophecy has been revealed."

It said no more, but just blinked nervously at him. He waited briefly, and then lost patience and yelled loudly at it in a threatening voice.

"Spit it out or I will show you the sharp end of this Twitch." Draig was always deeply concerned when he heard that prophecies were being proclaimed. He knew that with the speaking, came the power to fulfil. He needed to know exactly what had been proclaimed, and if it concerned him or not. Why had the prophecy not come through him? Was he not the greatest Zaurlock in the earth?

The HuverWort convulsed once in nervous response. It then steadied itself, as though collecting its thoughts, and began to speak, in Eastlander tongue, the words of the prophecy exactly as it had heard it from the mouth of the Gimp.

As it spoke, the strangest phenomenon took place. When each word was spoken it miraculously etched itself into the rock wall behind Draig.

Both he and Megan turned to witness the incredible feat of magic that was unfolding before their very eyes.

Draig's eyes widened as each word appeared, and the meaning of the prophecy started to dawn on him.

When the HuverWort finally finished his recitation, the finished proclamation filled the entire wall. Draig read, and then reread the words aloud:

"This is the prophecy that I the holy one speak this day. The shroud between earth and deep earth has been rent. Evil has pervaded the earth through one who seeks it wrongly. It brings with it persecution of my innocent, who I have now chosen as the vessel to right the wrong. Seek out the Stone of Deliverance, for it belongs with my innocent. In her hand, it shall cause the shroud to be restored, and evil to once again be contained. Seek and find the Stone in the holy city."

Megan also read the words. They were just as Rasita had said. This was her confirmation miraculously presented. She was the chosen one. Her heart leaped within her with such a sense of deep and satisfying joy as she had never felt before. All at once, the revelation became clear. She had to escape this tyranny which Draig was inflicting upon her. There were vital actions which she must take to preserve the future of mankind. Had she become so important? The black Zaurlock was no longer the feared dominator she perceived him to be, even a few minutes before. She was the chosen one, and she would be delivered out of this oppression, and freed to be outworked with the prophecy. It was written, and now it was proclaimed. With the speaking, the power of the prophetic words had released their own intrinsic power. Hey were self perpetuating and would fulfil their purpose. She sat back, revelling in her newly found confidence. She was still physically trapped, both within the gilded cage, and within the beastly cloak of a panther, but she was immeasurably free inside.

Draig turned away from the truth presented on the wall, his deep anger rising up and flaring into an uncontrollable state. He vented his rage on the HuverWort, lashing out and striking the small minion with a bolt of raw power which shot from the end of the Searing Twitch. Flying sporadically in its effort to flee, it blindly hit the opposite wall with a resounding thud, and fell motionless to the floor. It did not move again. Draig did not react at all to the minion's demise.

He turned to Megan to further vent his unabated fury. The Searing Twitch finding her skin over and over. She howled as each agonizing contact sent shooting pains upwards along her spine. It felt like a hot burning shaft piercing the base of her brain. Even after she had collapsed into a comatose state, he continued his torture. He was like one possessed. He would destroy her so that the prophecy would never be perpetrated.

Chapter 9

The Gimp stood and followed Nah back to the burned out camp fire site. He started to collect tinder to make a fire for their breakfast when Nah stopped him. "Come my friend, sit with me, and I will tell you about something extraordinary which happened last night."

Quan squatted down opposite Nah with his elbows resting on his knees. He gave his full attention to him, and waited for him to share his tale.

"Last night we were spied on by Draig's HuverWort. It had melded itself into a rock as camouflage, so we would not suspect its presence. This means that it heard every thought and word that we spoke, and that it has related it all back to Draig. This is relatively unimportant." Quan nodded thoughtfully without interrupting, allowing the white Zaurlock to continue. "The most important and amazing event that occurred was that you were used to prophesy."

The look of sheer bewilderment on Quan's face told Nah that he had no recollection of the episode at all. Nah was not surprised by this. It was common in those who prophesy as they are simply being used as a vessel by a greater power.

"What did I say?" Quan was tentative, but eager at the same time.

Nah repeated the prophesy word for word, as the Gimp

listened intently. When Nah had finished, Quan remained silent, his head bent in deep reflection. Finally, he raised his head and spoke. "This surely means that we are on the right path. This journey to Alabasteil is indeed ordained by the Holy One, and we have raised the interest of the black Zaurlock."

"Yes, my friend, we have to make haste to reach Alabasteil. The Council of Rah has to be informed and consulted. They need to give us guidance in regard to the Stone of Deliverance. We have no time to waste."

After Nah had carefully scribed the words of the prophecy onto a scroll, they quickly broke camp, and continued on their journey to the holy city. They travelled constantly, from first light, to when the last vestiges of the day were leaving the western sky.

One night, when they had made camp just off the main travel way, and were preparing to sleep, they were suddenly alerted to the presence of danger. Quan sensed it first. His keen eyesight caught the small movement, as a dark shadow disappeared behind a tree, just a short distance from their camp.

Sagent Nah had been expecting some sort of resistance given the gravity of their mission. He had been surprised that they had come this far unhindered. He engaged his ether vision and scanned the area. Three shapes were being exposed under the intense light rays coming from his closed eyes. Pointing to their position, Nah drew his sword and stood to his full seven feet height, ready to defend and do battle.

Quan reached to the depths of his being to touch his battle ire. It flared within him in eagerness. Even with his small stature the Gimp looked fearsome, and appeared much larger than he actually was. His bow was raised in assault position, with his first arrow notched in readiness, as he swept the area indicated by Nah. He looked for the first sign of attack. His short dagger was held between his teeth.

The shapes moved with an unearthly swiftness, which told them these were not human assailants, but something more sinister.

Quan sensed others behind him and alerted Nah. They changed positions to the classic back to back defence stance. Three more attackers abruptly appeared. Scaled forms with glowing red eyes attacked them from both sides. Nah swung his sword in a backhanded arc taking off the head of one of the creatures. It screamed its death wail, and disappeared completely giving the human adversaries confidence that this foe could, at least be killed.

The Gimp crouched down in readiness, as another assailant charged him in a full frontal attack. Quan was not distracted by the fact that his antagonist had no legs, as he deftly loosed an arrow, finding its mark in the scaly throat of the advancing creature. It gurgled in pain clutching at the shaft protruding from its neck, its red eyes going dim, before it evaporated into nothingness. Another flashing blade aimed at his head, narrowly missed its mark. Quan took the dagger from between his teeth, and, with a loud battle cry, he stabbed the next aggressor between its bony ribs, piercing its heart. His battle ire flaring fiercely, the Gimp gave himself over completely to it. He attacked the next victim with gusto, disposing of him skilfully.

Nah moved with grace in his war dance, belying the lethal potency of his well honed battle manoeuvres. The two remaining attackers came at him both at once, an onslaught of flashing razor sharp blades. They split up at the last moment, to try to confuse their intended victim. With practiced efficiency, Nah slid his blade across the neck of the closest one, removing his head completely, while pivoting around to thrust home his sword into the back of the other, as it passed him by. In similar fashion, they both disappeared from sight leaving the victors still in the back to back position. They were breathing heavily from the effort of the skirmish.

Nah dropped down on one knee with his elbow on the other, his breath becoming more regular. "As if we needed it, this is further verification that we are on the right path Quan."

"What do you think they were? I have never encountered the likes of them before." Quan looked around for any remaining evidence of the creatures. There was nothing. Even their weapons had vanished completely.

"If we take heed of the words of the prophecy, that the shroud between the earth and deep earth has been breached, then we can only assume that these beings were from below and sent to stop us from getting to Alabasteil, and, to the Stone of Deliverance." Nah stopped and considered his own words thoughtfully.

They slept fitfully that night unable to rest peacefully after the disruption earlier. They took turns to stand watch while the other slept.

Their passage over the following days was uneventful. Finally they were approaching the outer boundaries of the holy city. As they rode wearily along the cobbled road, the city gates came into view. They were immense, and imposing, emitting a dazzling white elegance which always impressed Nah afresh, no matter how many times he visited.

The city itself was vast and commanding. It was embedded into the mountain side, its soaring walls with the high turrets and ramparts were all constructed of the finest white alabaster. It shone resplendently in the morning sunlight. The entire city looked down from its vantage point, as if it were somehow living and able to see those that approached along the ribbon of white cobbled stone road, which wound its way up to the bridge and the city gates beyond.

As they drew near to the spiked drop gate on the city side of the bridge, they were stopped by the city guards. One of them recognized Sagent Nah from his regular pilgrimages in previous years, and admitted them without further scrutiny.

"Where can I find the elect at this time of day?" he asked the guard who was locking the gate behind them.

"They will be in prayer in the main sanctuary until noon today, but I suggest that you can go to their palace quarters and wait for them there. I am sure that you will be welcomed by the servants who will provide you with refreshments while you wait." The guard nodded respectively toward the Zaurlock, but looked down his nose at the Gimp beside him.

Quan ignored the snub. He was used to people looking suspiciously at him. He did not particularly need anybody's acceptance or approval. He kicked his donkey in the flanks, and moved off not bothering to look back.

They easily found the palace quarters as Nah knew his way around the city well. The servants were more than accommodating as the guard had suggested. They even welcomed Quan who was pleased not to be discriminated against, for once. Their guestrooms were prepared, and their mounts were stabled, fed and groomed.

A much welcomed lunchtime meal of beef and potato broth with freshly baked bread and wine was served. They sat with the many acolytes resident there at an enormously long table seating some one hundred and fifty people. The administrator had been informed of their arrival, and had, after reading the short letter hastily quilled by Sagent Nah, scheduled an urgent appointment with Popus Claiborne, the Chief Minister of the Council of

Rah.

The Council consisted of thirty one councillors, all of which were over the one hundred year old pre-requisite age, and had passed the extreme testing required for acceptance into the guild. Each was exceptionally well educated in all things enchanted. Every one brought extraordinary talents and special gifts, which in concert made the Council of Rah a formidable force for good within the kingdom. The Council dealt with matters of magic, which were seen to be in breach of their very clear and well defined statutes. Their reputation for implementing swift, and in extreme cases, lethal remedial action was legendary. The Council had existed and survived with an unblemished record for over seven hundred years. The constitution laid down at inception had remained unaltered in that entire time. Eons of statutory practice had set the laws and the implementation of their enforcement in concrete. Specially trained enforcers were sent forth with predefined solutions to remedy infractions. In the extreme cases assassins were assigned to manage the more recalcitrant transgressors.

Nah's brief furlough was cut short when he was summoned to an emergency meeting of the Council. They had agreed to sit out of their usual hearing times when Claiborne had read Nah's letter.

He went immediately to the Council chambers, and was admitted as soon as he arrived. He was ushered into a meeting room filled with council members.

Popus Claiborne sat at the head of the long table. His large frame sat well in the stately and ornate leader's chair. Everything about him spoke of wisdom and authority. This was accentuated by his long white hair and beard. Dressed in a silken white robe, his only jewellery was the gold medallion of office, which hung regally around his neck. His eyes were the dominating feature of his strong face. They were piercing in their intensity, and never wavered or averted from the object of his attention. All the other thirty councillors were present, and sat fifteen each side of the table. A single chair was vacant at the opposite end to Popus Claiborne. Nah was directed to sit.

No formal introductions were necessary as Nah knew each of those present, and they knew him. All had read the letter.

"Sagent Nah has brought to our attention a very grave matter." Popus opened the meeting without any pomp or ceremony.

"Each of you has read his letter. I will now ask white Zaurlock Nah to tell us more."

Standing to his feet Nah cleared his throat and began. "My brother Draig, the black Zaurlock has, I believe, sought after and acquired attributes of magic which are against the code of conduct set down by this governing body, and in fact against humanity itself. He has submitted to, and I believe acts, as agent for evil entities not of this world."

He paused to clear his throat once more.

The members of the council shared grave looks, and some heads were shaking in disbelief. Popus remained impassive but his jaw was set firmly: his face a portrait of consternation.

"As a result of this unlawful relationship, he has been acting in what I can only describe, as an insane manner. He has done the most unimaginable and despicable act. He has abducted King Henrik's only daughter."

Gasps of shock and astonishment were heard around the table. Voices rose in shouts of outrage. Fists were shaking, and the room filled with uncustomary hostility.

Popus leapt to his feet and demanded order.

The room immediately became quiet. He continued after a brief and challenging scrutiny of the faces in the room.

"I too, am outraged, but we must keep order and hear all that Nah has to say. Please continue Sagent."

"I would like to say that the abduction was the worst of it, but Draig has even eclipsed that act by delving deeper into the black arts. He has morphed the princess into animal form."

The room was stunned into silence. They had never before experienced such flagrant disregard for the law. This was akin to an all out declaration of spiritual war. Many wanted to immediately begin strategy to apprehend the rebel Draig. Voices were again raised in protest.

"Silence." Popus again stood to his full height, and stared threateningly at those present. "If you cannot come to order and remain silent, I will clear the room, and continue this meeting with Sagent Nah alone. This is my last and final warning."

The room was instantly muted. No one, including Nah looked directly at Popus, but averted their eyes.

"You may now continue without interruption Nah."

"Draig morphed Princess Megan into a fox. Fortunately, she

was returned to human form through the sacrifice of one Rasita Darilus, who himself was the result of an experiment gone wrong. Draig had dabbled with a primitive form of vulpine morph spell. Rasita graciously gave up his opportunity to return to human form to allow the princess to be restored. They had to use the creature force of both of them to return only one. Rasita was a young man studying to be a Zaurlock convert under the tutelage of Draig."

The assembly had lapsed into a more reflective and sombre mood when confronted with the bravery and nobility of the young man Rasita Darilus.

Nah continued, "Now I must tell you of the most worrisome aspect of my report. On our journey here we were attacked by beings from the underworld. They were strange shadowlike creatures, with scaled bodies and glowing red eyes. They worked as an organized squad. I believe that they came specifically to hinder, if not stop our coming here. We managed to defeat them, but the message was clear."

Pausing briefly to allow them to digest what he had said so far, he continued with the final and most important part of his discourse.

"There has been a prophecy proclaimed."

A proclamation of prophecy marked a significant event in history for those in the service of enchantment and the art of magic. The looks of dismay, which were so prevalent just minutes ago, changed to looks of excitement, even joy at the prospect of a prophecy. There did not even consider whether the prophecy was good or bad. It was a prophecy, and cause for celebration.

Nah was appalled that they were becoming sidetracked by the event, rather than concentrating on the important issue at hand. Festivity could come later once all is resolved, and Megan is safe again. His thoughts went briefly to her. He wondered where she was, and he hoped that he would be in time to save her further abuse from his deranged brother.

"What are the words of the prophecy?" asked Popus.

Nah produced a scroll onto which he had penned the words exactly as he had heard them. He rolled out the scroll and began speaking the prophecy boldly to the eager listeners.

"This is the prophecy that I the holy one speak this day. The shroud between earth and deep earth has been rent. Evil has pervaded the earth through one who seeks it wrongly. It brings with it persecution of my

innocent who I have now chosen as the vessel to right the wrong. Seek out the Stone of Deliverance for it belongs with my innocent. In her hand, it shall cause the shroud to be restored and evil to once again be contained. Seek and find the Stone in the holy city."

Popus Claiborne rose to his feet.

"We have heard the very grave report from Zaurlock Nah. We will remain here in session until we have produced a solution to this heinous list of misdemeanours perpetrated by the black Zaurlock Draig."

He continued addressing Nah directly, "White Zaurlock Sagent Nah we thank you for your diligence in reporting this seriously significant matter to the Council. We now dismiss you so that we can concentrate on the resolution. We will advise you as soon as consensus is reached."

Nah, bowing and leaving the scroll with them, retreated through the door closing it behind him.

Chapter 10

Evil has pervaded the earth through one who seeks it wrongly. It brings with it persecution of my innocent, who I have now chosen as the vessel to right the wrong.

Megan regained consciousness behind the protective curtain hidden deep within her mind. She silently thanked Sagent Nah again for his training; it was the only thing that had saved her from completely going insane. The terror and the intensity of the pain Draig inflicted on the limbs and torso of her panther body would have been too much for her young mind. She opened her eyes, carefully scanning the room for his whereabouts. He was nowhere to be seen. She tried to move, but the pain racked her body so much that she lay still, unsure of what to do next. Looking down, she observed that even though it had been tortured her panther body appeared fully morphed. It was larger than she had noticed the day before. The black fur was thick and covered the entire body. It shone like polished ebony, apart from the welts left from the series of inflictions made by Draig with that dreadful rod. Large red and painful sores and burns disfigured the torso and limbs. Its powerful muscular frame looked strong even as it lay on its side in pain on the cage floor. The length of the body astounded Megan; it must have been as long as a man was tall. The hind legs were larger than the front ones. Long razor like claws retracted into the large padded paws. She noticed that a lengthy tail had been added since she last looked. There were no mirrors this morning so she could not see her panther face, but she imagined how it might look. She remembered the animal that was presented to her father in court. She imagined that her head was small compared to her large body. She had noticed in the mirror the day before that the locket was still around her neck, although it was fitting tightly to her throat. Her eyes were probably emerald green, and, as she moved her mouth around, she felt the long fangs and whiskers. She flicked her cup shaped ears, but could not ascertain exactly what they looked like.

She would not venture back into her panther mind yet. If she could feel the pain so intensely behind the shield of her mental haven, it must be agonizing. Somehow she had to protect the panther body; it was her way back to becoming human again.

She remembered the prophecy, and the comfort that she felt, as she meditated on the words. There was definitely something supernatural afoot here, and she was undeniably part of it. She recalled that the words were miraculously etched into the solid rock wall behind her. She tried to move her panther head around to again read the words which offered such solace. The panther howled in pain as she inched her way around. After some time, she managed to see it clearly. The words were still there. She read, and reread them, drawing on the comfort and reassurance that they produced in her. The brief respite was cut short as Draig entered the room.

His face was contorted into a vicious scowl. He had spent the entire night without rest. His doom had been proclaimed, and he felt cheated. He knuckled his reddened eyes, and looked again at the wall, secretly hoping that the words would have disappeared overnight. His dismay was obvious as he saw the etchings had deepened, and taken on a feint red glow rather than diminishing. He had used the Twitch without restraint on Megan. This usually meant that she would not have survived mentally, and his unbridled issue of the searing magic should have also damaged the physical body beyond healing. Somehow she withstood her demise. The morphed animal was close to death. He could hear its laboured breath as it lay on the cage floor. He had to finish the task. If he let her live, she would unleash untold power for good. The prophecy said as much.

He knew of the Stone of Deliverance. He had seen firsthand its discovery while completing his study of alphawizardry at the holy city, nearly a century ago. It was an ancient artefact steeped in magic. Lying undiscovered and buried for centuries, until the Council of Rah unearthed it, in their diggings within the holy city. By chance, it was uncovered during a foundation excavation for their new temple. As the worker was about to swing his scraper spade into the soil, it was miraculously halted midway through the arc. The worker stepped back, as the implement burned up while still suspended in the air. The ground then opened up by itself, and the Stone rose to head height. It had shone with brilliance so bright, that they all had to shield their eyes, or be blinded by the intensity of the rays being emitted from its centre. A scroll, covered in ancient runes and inscriptions unravelled from beneath the Stone, and floated by itself in the air. After a considerable time, the brilliance faded, and the Stone was taken down into the secret catacombs beneath the existing old temple, and has remained there since.

Yes, he had to finish Megan. It was crucial to his survival. He sensed it within himself. It was as if the hourglass of his life had been turned upside down, and the sand of his existence was progressively slipping away without him being able to stop it. He would not allow that to continue. He would change fate and prevent the prophecy from happening.

He silently cursed himself for disposing of the HuverWort in his anger. He could use his little talisman now to spy on any developments occurring at the holy city, especially with regard to The Stone. Never mind, he had decided to finish off the catalyst, and that would be sufficient to stymie any further advancement before it got started.

The decision made, he turned menacingly toward the cage. The prophetic words inscribed on the wall behind it confronted him once again. He reacted in anger without thinking. Gathering together the most powerful devastative magic in his arsenal, he loosed twin bolts of Zaurlock flames from his outstretched hands. The shafts crackled potently in the air before reaching the wall. The magical force that was released would usually have the power to reduce the hard rock surface of the wall to molten lava, thus achieving his purpose of obliterating the cursed words from his sight. The force hit the wall with a resounding crash, but instead of the anticipated eradication, the words remained, and the entire force of the blast was repelled back at its perpetrator. Draig was hit in midsection by the fist of raw power. He reeled backward, slamming hard against the opposite rock wall. The breath was completely knocked out of him, and he lurched forward slumping down on the floor. Had he not spent time through last night weaving and casting a strong defensive shield around him, he would not have been able to withstand the onslaught. He would have been annihilated. There was enough devastative magic released to char a defenceless victim to a cinder.

Dragging himself to a sitting position, he waited until his breathing returned to normal. Things were certainly not as they had been. He was not used to being on the receiving end. He rested, licking the wounds of his dented confidence. He must not react in anger again. Every time he did, it did not go well for him. He chided himself and turned his calmer thinking to the grisly task of removing Megan from the equation.

She had witnessed the failed attempt by Draig's assault on the Words. It gave her confidence to see that he was not all powerful, that he could fail. The look on his face gave her some cause for alarm though. Her panther body was in a weakened state and vulnerable to his evil intentions. Had he quickened to the possibility that she was the chosen one in the prophecy? That revelation would spell her demise at his hand. He would not want her to be alive to play her part in bringing him to heel. Surely the greater power for good, who had released the prophetic words, could also release her from this end. She would be of no use if she were dead.

He had regained his strength and composure. He stood, and began moving her way, dusting himself off as he came. He did not take his evil eyes from her. The wheels of his sinister mind turned as he glared at her menacingly. He stopped directly in front of the door of her cage. Still staring at her with unblinking eyes, he deliberately drew back his robes revealing a cruel dagger still in the sheath attached to his belt. He waited for her eyes to see the weapon before unsheathing it, and bringing it up in front of him. The light reflected off the sharp point of the long curved blade.

"Unfortunately for you, your time has come Megan. You have proven to be too dangerous to me alive. You will never fulfil the prophecy, for I still control your fate."

Megan knew that what he was saying was really how it was. She was vulnerable and weak and unable to defend herself. He could, at his leisure dispose of her, and she could do nothing to prevent it.

Her only consolation was that she was now certain that she was the one referred to in the prophecy. Something instinctive within her seemed to confirm it. No doubt remained, she was the chosen one. Keeping that in the forefront of her thinking emboldened her to step back into her corporeal panther mantle. She needed to at least attempt to save herself. She could not do anything sheltered in her inner haven. As she drew back the curtain, the pain struck her like tightly closed fist. She braced herself against the sheer torture of the sudden exposure to her physical self. She heard herself scream with a blood curdling howl. She tried to stand, but the pain prevented her from doing so. Surely this was not the end. Surely the Holy One would rescue her, did she not have a greater purpose and calling.

Draig, still brandishing the lethal weapon he had chosen to end her life also took up the Twitch in his other hand. Had he not caused enough pain already, without inflicting one last onslaught of torture on an already enfeebled body? Was he so cowardly as to think that the panther body could somehow still harm him? He could see plainly that his previous relentless barrage of pain had permanently disabled even the powerful panther. He had no compassion at all. He was only intent of satisfying some sick bloodlust which dominated his worthless life. He raised the dagger to trip the latch on the cage door. Megan braced herself for the worst. She would not beg. She would die with dignity.

As soon as the dagger made contact with the gold latch a loud, deep voice resonated forth in a deafening warning.

"Do not touch my chosen one."

Draig froze. The voice carried with it an ominous sense of omnipresence and deity. He moved back warily from the cage, the words on the wall came into his full view. They began to glow. The intensity increased until they burst in to a blinding radiance, turning blood red as a deep thunder like rumble sounded forth.

Megan felt an instant release from pain. An amazing feeling of peace overwhelmed her. She saw the welts on her torso and limbs disappearing before her eyes. Her strength returned to full power, and she leapt to her feet standing aggressively with her head lowered. She faced Draig and snarled, baring her long fangs. Her emerald green eyes flared with hatred.

He recoiled from her, backing up defensively and no longer looking like the aggressor. The dagger fell from his hand.

A cloud of energy moved across from the wall of words. The latch on the gate released and the door swung open. Megan felt a strong but pleasant sensation in her throat, about where the locket would be positioned. It must have been the seal which Draig had placed on the locket being broken.

She moved closer to the open door of the cage projecting her head into the open space; she never took her livid eyes from Draig. A low menacing growl rumbled up from deep in her chest and up into her throat. She bared her long fangs in a vicious snarl, making her lethal intentions clear.

He backed away further until the wall behind him stopped his retreat.

Megan leapt forward using her strong hind legs like a springboard. In one lithe movement she was upon him, her front paws placed on the wall each side of his face. Her beastly countenance so close to his, that he could feel the heat of her panting hot breath.

Instinctively he raised the Twitch, which he still had in his other hand, and shoved it hard against Megan's ribcage. She screamed with pain and drew back, raking his face with her razor sharp claws as she went.

It was his turn to scream as the pain shot through his shredded and bleeding face. His hand covered in blood as he pressed it against the rented flesh that was once his cheek. His shaggy beard turned red and matted with his own blood.

Megan prepared to pounce once more, and this time she would tear out his throat. She had given over to the panthers urges without attempting to control it. She had been oppressed for too long. Now was the time for retribution.

Then she heard the voice from the wall again sounding forth. *"This is not my desire."*

Megan somehow held back the aggression which threatened to explode into vengeful and murderous fury. She restrained the panther, and quelled her own urge for revenge, drawing herself back away from him, she waited. She still eyed him savagely and continued to snarl, sounding a low rumble of aggression from her deep chest.

The words still glowing with red energy were miraculously extracted out of the wall and came together forming up in the shape of a huge ramrod.

Thrusting forth the ramrod of words smashed through the

outside wall of rock reducing it to rubble. A gaping hole was left, where sold rock had been. The bright sunlight flooded into the room filling it with bright, radiating warmth.

Megan took one last threatening look at the black Zaurlock before leaping through the gap and into the freedom beyond.

* * *

Late in the day following Nah's session with the Council of Rah, he was again summoned to the chambers. He was guided into a smaller meeting lounge area where Popus Claiborne sat waiting for his arrival. He came to his feet as Nah entered the room.

"Welcome Nah." His face remaining serious to match the gravity of the situation.

After they were seated, Popus opened the conversation immediately, dispensing with any of the usual cordialities.

"We have deliberated long and hard in regard to all that you have told us." His expression and tone of voice conveyed his concern.

"We have reached a unanimous decision." He came straight to the point. "The Stone of Deliverance must be released into the hand of Megan in accordance with the prophecy. She is undoubtedly the chosen one. We considered making the princess come to us here and leaving the Stone undisturbed. But as time is of vital importance, we have agreed that the Stone should be taken to her. We will not take any direct action against Draig the black Zaurlock at this time. The Stone of Deliverance in the hand of the chosen one has the power to resolve all the issues. We will not interfere with the outworking of the prophecy."

Nah remained silent and did not offer comment.

The Council leader continued, "There are however, certain conditions around the release of the Stone. When it was discovered, miraculous happenings accompanied the unearthing. As the Stone rose out of the diggings, a scroll also appeared. It was later revealed to be a set of conditions under which the Stone can be moved from the holy city." He paused, scrutinizing Nah's face to see that he comprehended fully what was being said.

Satisfied, he continued, "In order for the Stone to be moved there has to be a designated 'Bearer of the Stone' who must undergo and pass certain tests to be able to successfully carry and convey the artefact to the chosen one."

Nah spoke for the first time. "Who can be a bearer?"

Popus did not reply immediately but gave consideration to his answer before responding. "It cannot be any body from the holy city."

This surprised Nah. He pursed his lips and raised his eyebrows slightly in response, as he had imagined that one of the councillors or even one of the appointed assassins would be the logical choice.

"Neither can it be a Zaurlock." He looked hard at Nah as he said it.

"Who then can qualify?"

"The scroll says that the bearer must initially be selected by the Stone itself. They must then pass the prescribed tests. If they fail, then another candidate is selected, and the process continues until the bearer is found."

"Is there not an easier way? This could take too much time. Megan could be in grave danger." Nah voiced his concern.

Popus looked doubtful, and at the same time concerned for Megan, but he said that was how it had to be and the rules were irrevocable.

Nah moved on resolutely.

"How does a stone select a candidate?" Nah was not so much sceptical, but he was more interested in the process.

"Clear and concise guidelines have also been included in the scroll. But basically the candidate comes before the Stone, and, if it glows green, then he or she has passed the first test."

"How soon can we start the selection process?" Nah was impatient to have what seemed to be an archaic procedure out of the way so he could begin Megan's rescue attempt.

"Do you have a suitable candidate in mind Nah?"

Sagent Nah realized almost immediately that he did not. Any of the ones which came to mind were back in the palace. He could not afford another two weeks of time to have them come to Alabasteil.

The only one he would trust and who was here right now with him, was the Gimp. Quan's integrity was indisputable and his capability to protect the Stone would be second to none. But how would the Council of Rah react to a Gimp as a candidate? Would they trust him with one of their oldest and most valuable relics and allow him to undertake such an important assignment?

Nah did not immediately suggest Quan for the task. He had not yet consulted him, and he also needed time to present his case to the Council in such a way, that they would grant his candidature.

"If I can produce a suitable candidate, can we then start the testing immediately?"

"I understand the urgency, so we will do all that is necessary to streamline the process to the shortest possible time." With that statement Popus concluded the meeting.

* * *

"Are you serious?" Quan smiled in disbelief. "Do you really think that they would let a Gimp anywhere near their precious relic? It is their most sacred and valuable possession. It is out of the question."

"Quan, please reconsider, this is of the highest importance, If I can have them agree, will you at least put yourself before the Stone and let it decide?"

"Good luck with the first part." Quan's good natured reply said that he would be willing.

Nah spent most of the remainder of the day convincing the Council to allow Quan to submit himself before the Stone. To get thirty one difficult people to agree to something of this significance was a feat which Nah could only attribute to the Holy One's divine intervention. But in the end they agreed.

Quan was taken to the inner sanctum deep within the myriad of rooms known as the catacombs. The Stone was kept securely and secretly there. They were all without their weaponry as the rules stated. All thirty one Council members and Sagent Nah accompanied him as witnesses to the outcome.

They entered through a large dome shaped atrium, which led into another more intimate rectangular area deeper within. The room had high ceilings, and ornate walls displaying ancient runes and markings. In the centre of the ceiling was a round aperture of a crystalline substance, which allowed the light to penetrate an otherwise dark room. The light coming through the crystal opening seemed brighter and more intense than just sunlight. Directly beneath the aperture sat a small altar. On the altar was The Stone of Deliverance. It was sitting on a modest wooden stand signifying humility. In front of The Stone lay a rolled up scroll tied around its centre with a thin leather lace. Smaller than Quan had imagined, it was about the size of a large grape. It had innumerable facets, which made looking directly at it taxing on the naked eye. The hues were constantly changing, taking in the full spectrum of colours. Even in the intense brightness of the light coming from above, the brilliance of The Stone made it clearly stand out. It even outshone the magnified sunlight.

Quan was directed to stand in front of the small altar facing The Stone.

All thirty one members linked hands in a circle around him. Nah was excluded from the ritual, but was allowed to remain in the room. Ancient words were repeated three times, and then the group fell silent and waited.

After only a short time, The Stone of Deliverance began to change colour. It started out with light green tinge, and it progressively darkened and altered until it became a deep emerald shade. A shaft of the marvellous green light emerged from the centre of the stone and focused on the breast of the Gimp.

Chapter 11

She loped along relishing her freedom. Her panther body had recovered and regained its full strength in the short time since her escape, and she was amazed at the speed at which she could move. Looking down at the ground as it sped past; she briefly increased her speed to go as fast as she could, just for the fun of it. She slowed down again to a walk and listened to her thoughts, as she padded majestically along the woodland trail.

Her escape from the oppressive Draig had been nothing short of miraculous. She was still faced with the prospect of perhaps never being able to revert to a human again. Rasita's hopeless situation was her case in point. He had missed a deadline to beat the first nightfall, and had paid the price of years of entrapment in the body of a fox. Would she share the same fate? How many deadlines had she missed?

Stopping at a grove of trees she observed the muted light produced by the sun sneaking peaks through the thick canopy above. A pond of fresh water looked appealing as she had acquired a huge thirst. Dropping to her underbelly at the edge of the water and lowering her head she lapped copious amounts of the sweet tasting liquid. Her thirst satisfied, she stretched out on the thick green grass and relaxed. After her traumatic few weeks, she appreciated the respite. Ignoring the thoughts that incessantly tried to invade her peace; she found the solitude of the place refreshing. At some point she must plan her future but just now she would put all those things on hold, past, present, and future, and just unwind. Her body glistened with a film of sweat from her recent exertion. The cool and gentle breeze caressed the length of her torso, and gave her such a sensation of delight, that she actually purred from deep in her throat. The sound of bees humming filled her ears, and through a gap in the canopy, she observed that the sky above was a cloudless expanse of blue. Peace enveloped her, and she felt that she could easily spend the rest of her life, right there. She lazily closed her eyes, but the thoughts persisted.

In her short time as a panther morph she had come to know some of the idiosyncrasies of the beast. She would ensure that she had fully mastered her feline mantle. If she was to be the chosen one, whether she was human or imprisoned within this creature, she knew that she had to fulfil her destiny. Her miraculous escape from certain death had changed her view on life dramatically. Her life was no longer her own.

It had not occurred to her that the panther may have thoughts of its own. She had no real way of finding out. It had acted in its own volition before, but was that just instinct or was a morphed panther different from a naturally occurring one? What she did know was that when she imposed her will on the beast it responded and did not resist her. She would explore the capabilities of the animal fully, and learn to use them to her best advantage; she may even be more effective in outworking her fate in this morphed state.

When it came to sustenance, she let go of control, and allowed the beast to act by instinct. It hunted and killed small animals and greedily devoured them to appease the hunger pangs. She was becoming inured to this aspect, and she tried to be pragmatic as she had little choice but to be an integral part of the events.

The animal could climb trees and perform acts of agility with ease, and she was astounded at the acute sense of smell, eyesight and hearing which she experienced. A sense of physical arrogance and supremacy filled her at times. She could control an extremely powerful and aggressive beast. What humbled and sobered her thoughts each time she found insight into her musings of power, were the words of the prophecy, and the fact that she had been delivered from death for a purpose.

She roused herself and stretched her long body. She needed

a place of shelter, and a period of time without distraction to plan her next move. As a black panther, she was at risk from just about everyone in the Eastlands. She would be hunted down as a threat to the safety of the kingdom inhabitants. She could not afford to be killed when she carried such a heavy burden of responsibility to rectify the rift between the two earths. The Hajus Woods would provide that place. She headed off with that destination in her mind.

* * *

Draig inspected his wounded cheek. It had started to heal with the help of his healing invocations, but there would always be an ugly scar to remind him of who had done this to him. He now had additional reason for vengeance. He could see that even with his superior power and talent, he had failed to enforce his will on Megan. She had somehow enlisted the aid of the Holy One. He reluctantly admitted to himself, that if he was to maintain his standing as the most powerful Zaurlock in the kingdom, he also had to have assistance. The prophecy could not, and would not, be fulfilled.

Shortly after Megan's escape Draig had relocated to his beloved Hajus Woods. His mountain cavern had been partially demolished in the escape and was in disarray. He did not want the constant reminder of his abject failure. He felt he could command greater control from within the Hajus Woods. On arrival back there, he cast a wide surveillance web across the entire forest area which would alert him, and monitor the movements of anyone entering or leaving.

The dual keys to the prophecy's fulfilment were, Megan herself, and The Stone of Deliverance. He had to eliminate, or at worst case control both. He could frustrate the process by preventing the Stone from getting into her hand. He could have used his HuverWort to spy covertly for him but he had denied himself that advantage. He again chided himself for his rashness in killing one of his best creations. Oh well he would prevail anyway. He was Draig, the black Zaurlock.

The shroud between the two earths had been torn enough to allow some of the lower earth's inhabitants to bleed into this realm. It seemed that this knowledge was now commonplace, with the prophecy being carelessly bandied about all over the kingdom. He would enlist some of these powerful subordinates to do his hack work, while he could be left to use his many talents and superior abilities to strategize and plan his rise back to power and domination. He would recruit six of the best Heinions into his service on a trial basis. They had just recently come through the shroud and into this earthly realm, and would work with him just for the pleasure of it. Their unusual attributes would be extremely useful in bringing his enemies to heel. He had only seen one in action since the renting of the shroud. It was impressive enough to convince him that he had to have a contingent of them on his side. They could move like streaking darkness with extreme speed and efficiency. Their appearance was truly frightening. The most distinctive feature about them was that they had no legs. The bottom half of their scaly bodies was made up of incorporeal shadows. They appeared to be very tall scaly skinned beings with glowing red eyes, and with mouths that grinned constantly, not having gums or lips exposing ugly sharpened skeletal teeth. Excellent warriors highly skilled in swordsmanship, they could cut down a man in seconds. He had heard that there were many of the heartless fiends already roaming the Eastlands in gangs looting and pillaging in the small isolated towns. Reports of rape and murder were coming in with more regularity. Yes he must have some of these.

If he could take possession of The Stone he would control the prophecy. He immediately began working on the construct of magic seeking spells which would give him control of The Stone.

His Heinions would be charged with the task of retrieving the artefact. He would give them unlimited authority to do whatever they desired to do in carrying out his demands. He almost pitied anyone who would stand in their way.

* * *

The tests were scripted exactly from the instructions laid down in the scroll. Quan had spent the best part of a full day submitting himself to the arduous testing by the Council members. He had passed every test, including one where he was placed in a room which had a set of squares symmetrically drawn on the floor in a tessellated pattern. He was given fifteen small stone cairns and asked to place them on the squares in any order that he wished. To pass the test every cairn had to be positioned exactly as per the directives within the scroll. If one was misplaced, or placed on a square which should have been left empty, he would fail. This was one of the hardest for the Gimp. At first he stood before the riddle perplexed. Drawing on his supernatural ken, he emptied his mind, allowing his inner being to take over. Without hesitation he placed all cairns in the correct positions. The Council was extremely impressed.

Another test involved a great degree of trust for Quan. He was asked to put his bare hand over a flame and leave it there until the required count was made. Initially he was sceptical, but he convinced himself that so far the Holy One had been with him, and that he could not fail him now. At the signal from the members he confidently put his hand over the naked flame and was surprised that it did not burn him. The members completed their count nodding approvingly.

On the morning of the following day Sagent Nah and Quan were called in to the chambers of the Council.

Popus greeted them both warmly and then offering them refreshments. Nah and Quan gave each other a surprised look at the leader's newly found respect for the Gimp.

"Well my friends, I have good news for you both. Quan has passed the test without spot or blemish. We had four other candidates who did not make it past the first test with The Stone. Quan, I can now tell you that you are officially The Bearer of the Stone."

The Gimp did not show outwardly his delight at being chosen for this most esteemed purpose. His impassivity was well received by Popus, who placed his hand on the Gimp's shoulder. He took Quan's other hand in his and shook it heartily.

"Nah at first light tomorrow in a dawn ceremony we will pass The Stone to Quan and you can both leave the city to fulfil your quest. We will be providing you with two of our best escorts to accompany you and help to ensure the safe passage of The Stone."

They left the audience with Popus in an elevated mood as they both felt that they were now making progress, and they could put into action their most critical pursuit, which was to save Megan. She was the chosen one and now that they had The Stone, they next needed to rescue her.

The ceremony took place at dawn the next morning, as stated by the leader of the Council and Quan received The Stone into his safekeeping. As the two most senior members, with gloved hands, placed the relic into the Gimp's open palms he felt a surge of supernatural pleasure rise up in him as he had never experienced before. He felt that he was being shined upon, and that he was in the exact place in time and history that he was supposed to be. This was his destined moment to place his stamp on history. His face softened, and such a look of peace radiated from his countenance that some of the members present bowed their heads, recognizing and sensing the presence of the Holy One, around and within, The Bearer of the Stone.

Quan slipped into a trancelike state. He raised The Stone heavenward and he again proclaimed a prophecy.

"This is the second prophecy that I the Holy One speak and proclaim this day. This Stone carries with it my blessing. My innocent waits on the Plain of Rescuse beyond the Valley of Bones. Adversity rises and resists my will, but it will wane, for The Stone shall be united with my innocent, and the battle is won in the worldly realm."

The assembled fell to their knees and worshipped.

* * *

The troop of four left Alabasteil setting a gruelling pace to be back within the boundaries of the Eastlands realm as soon as was physically possible.

The second prophecy gave them the direction they needed. The Valley of Bones lay to the north of the kingdom, so they would reach it sooner. Time was incredibly important and could not afford to be squandered. Lives and potentially kingdoms were at risk every moment that The Stone was not in the hand of the chosen one.

The rent in the shroud was of grave concern. How many of the evil inhabitants of the deep earth had already escaped, no one could fathom. One of those fiends on the loose in the Eastlands realm would be enough to cause concern, as no tried and tested defence against them had been established. Apart from their skirmish on the way to Alabasteil, they were an unknown quantity. At least they knew that they could be killed.

As a precaution, Quan had hidden The Stone in a small leather bag and inserted it in the ear of his donkey attaching a drawstring for retrieval. It was obscured from sight by the profusion of hair in his donkey's ear. He spoke a calming charm into the donkey's other ear so that the leather bag would, through magic not irritate the animal into revealing its unorthodox hiding place. Before leaving Alabasteil, Quan had been given a lesson on what he, as the 'Bearer of the Stone' could do with respect to handling the relic. This was within protocol. He did not even share this stealth move with the others, as it was better that he alone knew where it was hidden. If they did not know it whereabouts, then they could not reveal it to others under pressure.

* * *

The Hajus Woods was much as she remembered. With its tangled tortured trees and dark crannies it definitely still felt like a bad place. But it suited her purposes right now. Hopefully no one else wanted to venture here. It was a refuge for outcasts. She was a pariah. Through no fault of her own she would be hunted down and possibly killed as a wild beast, without having any chance to defend herself verbally. Yes, the Hajus Woods was ironically the safest place for her to be at this time.

She found a small cave set into the side of a rocky hillock. It would suffice as a shelter from the wind and rain, and she judged that it was situated in about the centre of the Woods. A small rivulet feeding into a still pond provided fresh water. After a cursory inspection inside she found that the cave was empty, but it had been occupied recently by another animal. There were remains of an unfinished kill lying on the cave floor, and a heap of leaves in one corner had the shape of a curled up animal pressed into them where it had slept. Her nose told her that the animal had the scent of a fox.

Could it possibly be Rasita? The thought hit her with a jolt. There were hundreds of foxes roaming the woods. If it was Rasita he would probably not come near her for fear of being eaten. She was about six times his size and weight. If his keen nose picked up her scent, he would naturally avoid returning to his cave home.

She did not have to wait long to find out if it was indeed Rasita, and how he would react. The fox must have approached the cave from upwind, for it did not immediately sense her presence. It padded its way silently in through the mouth of the cave holding a freshly killed rodent between its jaws. Megan sat regally on her haunches and waited. Even if it was not Rasita, she was now unwilling to give up her new abode, especially to an animal of lesser weight and size than herself.

The fox stopped dead, the rodent falling from its mouth. It started to immediately take evasive action and flee back out of the cave when Megan cried out in fox language. "Rasita it's me, Megan."

The slight hesitancy in the fox's retreat told Megan that is really was her friend. He looked at the huge panther intently and could not believe his eyes as he recognized the gold locket around the neck of the beast.

"Megan, is that really you?"

"Rasita, it is me. It's a long story but it truly is me."

* * *

"How touching," Draig whispered quietly to himself. His distaste for the sentimental scene he was witnessing was very obvious.

These two fools have finally connected with each other. He had known that Rasita was occupying the cave. His surveillance web had picked up his movements earlier that day and Draig had been concentrating on observing him. He was surprised and delighted to see his nemesis Megan obliviously walk right in to his sphere of ethereal influence. He subconsciously raised his hand to touch the healing wound on his face as he dwelt on her foolhardy error. She was clearly not aware that this was his domain. He ruled here, and this presented him with the perfect opportunity to even the scores. He thought to himself that someone was looking after him and it was definitely not the Holy One.

* * *

Megan explained to Rasita in great detail all that had happened to her since she had last seen him. The last time they had seen each other was when she had waved from her bedroom window. She left nothing untold, including the episodes of torture inflicted by Draig in his madness.

Shaking his head in disbelief and chagrin, Rasita's heckles rose on his back and neck. He spoke forcefully, his voice filled with anger and outrage. "You have been treated shamefully. You have done nothing to deserve this. I will find some way to avenge this wrongdoing. Draig will not be absolved from this, ever. I will hunt him down and kill him myself." Finishing his short tirade, he sat breathing heavily from the torrent of emotion flowing from within him.

Megan was taken aback by his spirited defence of her, and the unexpected and passionate response, that had gushed forth from her friend.

She moved closer to him placing her head over his neck, and her large paw around his front legs, in what was the closest thing she could manage as a hug. He responded just as warmly and snuggled his head against her strong shoulders. After a few minutes they parted their embrace. She noticed the tears which had welled up in Rasita's eyes. He made no attempt to hide his emotion and sat back on his haunches looking at her. His eyes went again to the locket around her neck.

"Megan, we could perhaps call the white Zaurlock with your locket. He can surely help us again."

"My locket was sealed by Draig when I was taken, but I think that the seal may have been broken when the cage door was unspelled. I remember feeling something happening with it. But I cannot open it. My paws are too cumbersome."

"Let me try. My mouth is small, and I can use my teeth to pry it open." Rasita moved closer to Megan and placing his front paws on her chest, he stood on his back legs easily reaching the locket with his mouth.

It was not as easy as he thought, but he persisted and the locket fell open releasing Gemma the Halopod.

The small being floated up and suspended herself in front of the panther. Her eyes darted intelligently from the panther to the fox and back again. Her quick perception astutely summed up the situation.

"Megan, what has he done to you?" She empathized with the ineffable pain that Megan had endured, and all the doubt and confusion she was feeling at being once again in the form of an animal. It was Gemma's turn to shed a tear in sympathy for Megan's plight.

"I need you to find Sagent Nah and bring him back here. Go now."

The Halopod obediently disappeared from their sight.

* * *

He watched the Halopod flash past him in its haste to do her bidding. Did she think that he would allow this to happen so easily? He did not need his little brother interfering with his plans. Draig raised his hand sweeping a capture spell in a wide arc. It reached the bounds of his surveillance web ahead of the Halopod's flight path. The small messenger was caught midflight, and magically encased in a small cage like aura.

"What is this? Help me somebody. I'm trapped." The small voice rang out on deaf ears. There was nobody there to hear, or to help. Draig drew his captive back to him slowly. There was no hurry; it was not going anywhere now.

Draig smiled wickedly as an idea suddenly dawned on him. They wanted Sagent Nah to come to them. He would accommodate them and find out what they really had in mind.

* * *

The panther and the fox waited expecting Sagent Nah to appear almost instantly as he had done on previous occasions. He did not come.

"This is strange," said Megan. "He always comes straight away. Why is it taking so long?"

As if her words were heard, a blurry shimmer faded in and out before shaping into the white image of Sagent Nah.

Relieved at the appearance Megan started immediately to tell him of her grievances.

She stalled her words as the image of the white Zaurlock faded out and in again. She was immediately suspicious as Nah had not spoken or even asked why she was a panther.

There was something wrong. It was the eyes. They did not have the same kindness emanating from them as did those of her white Zaurlock.

"What is wrong princess?" The white image spoke for the first time.

Megan was now unsure, as the voice was that of Sagent Nah.

'Nothing really," she responded still looking intently at him. The scent of Draig came strongly to her sensitive nose.

"Tell me what you plan to do next," his blunt enquiry was not well received by the panther, who realizing his real identity, bared her long fangs in a vicious snarl. The fox also sensing the black Zaurlock's presence bravely leapt toward the image sinking his sharp teeth into the fleshy part of Draig's leg.

The Zaurlock yelled in pain, quickly retreating as the panther rose up to her full height and aggressively advanced in his direction her eyes flashing threateningly. She crouched ready to pounce.

He disappeared just before she made her charge. The fox's grip was shaken off as the Zaurlock disassembled.

They sat breathing quickly, allowing the tension of the moment to abate before speaking again.

"That was really disturbing. Draig is very deceptive and we need to be more diligent." Rasita spoke first.

"My concern is for Gemma my Halopod. She must have been intercepted on her way to Sagent Nah." Megan tensed at the thought of her little helper being held prisoner by her past tormentor. The empty locket lay open as it hung from her neck.

She now had one more reason to ensure that she firstly survived, and that she did everything on her power to become the powerful person that the prophecy portrayed. She would right the wrongs.

Chapter 12

Their ugliness even caused Draig to recoil. He had summoned the six Heinions to his cave home in the Hajus Woods.

They floated around in an impatient line as he called each one individually to come before him to be recruited into his service.

Draig could not get used to their constant and deathly grin and shifty eye movements. It made it difficult to ascertain whether they were serious, or having some sort of private joke at his expense. Nevertheless, they would be a formidable force for him to control and outwork his plans for ascension.

Their lack of legs made it easy for them to move around silently. Draig chuckled dryly to himself; at least he did not have to provide them with boots. His mirth quickly vanished as he finished recruiting the last of his scaly soldiers. He commanded them leaving no doubt who was in charge. "Your first assignment is to steal The Stone of Deliverance and bring it to me." He waited for their response.

As they did not answer promptly enough he released from his right hand a stun charge of Zaurlock's power. It went streaking through their midsections, causing an extremely painful stabbing sensation to tear at their innards.

Their howls rose as a torturous chorus before they answered

in unison. "Yes Mighty One. We will do your bidding."

Draig kept his hand visible so as to reinforce his threat and authority.

"Go now. The seeking spell is released and it will guide you to The Stone. Do not rest until you have it."

They speedily floated away passing effortlessly through the cave wall, leaving him alone.

He stepped back, wincing as the pain in his leg reminded him of the fox's sharp teeth. He gave himself a mental note not to try and be so realistic next time he wanted to pretend to be someone else. He had donned the whole physical charade in the hope that they would believe he was in fact Sagent Nah, and reveal some important things which would assist him in his quest for total domination. It had backfired badly. He had not counted on the fact that animal morphs had all the keen senses of their natural counterparts. How could there still be things for him to learn after three hundred years?

He was satisfied that there was nothing further that he needed to do right now. Megan could wait. Once he had possession of The Stone things would be very different. He would draw out the tremendous authority and powers contained in the holy relic, and add it to his already formidable arsenal.

Now just wait he told himself. But patience was never his strong point.

* * *

They set up camp on the third day of their return journey from Alabasteil. The mounts were hobbled and fed. Talk was limited to generalities and necessity as they were all exhausted from the hectic pace they had set since before dawn that morning. The evening meal was simple, which they consumed listlessly, and all, apart from the one escort designated to take the first watch were asleep before their heads had hit the sleeping rolls.

Nah was woken in the night by the escort. It was his turn to stand watch. He took his position standing at the camp's edge. As his mind cleared of the grogginess of sleep his thoughts went to the extraordinary events which had happened at Alabasteil. Quan had surprised even himself with his faultless result in the testing. Nah smiled to himself as he thought how the Holy One was guiding both he, and the Gimp. He had chosen Quan to accompany him. It was not by chance that he was willing and available to join him. Now they had The Stone of Deliverance in their care. When he had first been schooled about the origin and eternal relevance of The Stone, he never in his wildest imaginings thought that he would be part of the making of history, as the real purpose of its existence came to the fore. He worried about the security of the relic. What would happen if it ended up in the wrong hands? It had been protected for years within the walls of Alabasteil, now it was exposed. The first prophecy has been proclaimed and now the purpose for The Stone has been made known to all and sundry. Did Quan as the Bearer have enough supernatural blessing to provide all the protection necessary for it to make it safely into the chosen ones hand? Perhaps he should have more faith. He knew that he was one to worry too much, and that most of the things he spent fretting over never really eventuated. He had not had a call from the Halopod. He worried over that. That could mean one of two things. Either Megan was safe, and did not need his help or she could not send for it. It was no use having The Stone if Megan the chosen one was not able to use it. He tried to rein in his fears. The Holy One had said in the second prophecy that He would prevail even with the expected adversity. He chided himself again for his lack of faith in the higher power and resolved not to worry unnecessarily.

Quan tapped him on the shoulder. Nah jumped at the sudden intrusion into his reverie. "Quan, you startled me. Is it your turn already?"

"No, I could not sleep so I thought I would come and talk with you."

"You are welcome my friend. Speaking with you is much better than thinking my own thoughts right now."

They sat beside each other looking out into the dark night.

Quan voiced his concern. "The real reason why I could not sleep is that I sense that there is danger pending. Others seek to have The Stone, and will try to use it for evil, rather than the good for which it was intended."

"It is strange that you say that Quan, as I have been also concerned for its security. The decision to travel as a small group in order to attract less attention sounded rational when we all decided that it was the best way, but I fear that we are only a few against an unknown adversary."

It was as if their talk about their fears and suspicions somehow brought them to into being. A sudden shadowy movement through the trees caught Quan's attention. He grasped Nah's elbow signalling his detection, and their need for silence. They rose to their feet in readiness for confrontation. They sensed more movement behind them. Their years of drill as soldiers came into play. Their weapons were drawn. Quan remained facing out into the night, while Nah turned back toward the campsite. The movement they had felt was from the two escorts who had also sensed the impending danger and woken instantly alert and ready to repel an attack.

The four now formed a circle protecting each other's backs. They were ready.

Nah sighted the first of the Heinions. A second and a third appeared soon after. Before long five of the ghostly attackers floated eerily about the fringe of the forest.

One of the two escorts whispered hoarsely at Nah. "What are these beings? I have never seen anything like this before. Are they human? They don't have any legs."

"Do not fear what you see. We have fought them before. They can be killed just like human foe." Quan's words gave them back their courage.

The four were tense and anxious to get on with the battle. Their blood was up. They were all seasoned warriors and they looked fearsome as they stood, weapons drawn and in aggressive battle stance.

One of the Heinions, who appeared to be their leader moved out of the pack and floated closer. It continued to move cautiously in their direction.

Quan's bow was drawn with his arrow aimed at the heart of the creature as it approached.

It stopped about halfway between its ranks, and them. Its grinning lipless mouth seemed to mock them. Its eyes glowed red as it floated just above the ground.

"We have come for The Stone of Deliverance," its eerie high pitched demand aimed at no one in particular.

Quan spoke strongly in response. "What is this Stone of Deliverance that you seek?"

"Do not play games with us Gimp. We know that you have The Stone and we will not leave without it. If you resist us you will die." The voice deepened as the threat was given.

Sagent Nah stood with his feet apart and his forearm raised horizontally across his line of vision. His fist clenched his sword, which was placed on his arm in readiness. It was pointing directly at the enemy.

He spoke his own warning back at them. "It is you who will die this day. We have killed you're like before, and we will kill you again if you do not withdraw immediately. You will be shown no quarter."

The Heinion leader looked unsure and swayed nervously from side to side. Its other fiendish cohorts behind him looked from one to the other, as if taking stock of their collective courage.

Drawing backwards without turning around the head Heinion spoke his retreating words with bravado. "Do not underestimate our strength or our guile Zaurlock. We will meet again, and you will not be so fortunate next time."

The five phantom like beings melded back into the darkness.

"Quan! Is The Stone safe?" Nah turned to him as soon as the last Heinion disappeared.

The Gimp immediately looked to his donkey. He could not see it. He thought that it must be obscured in behind the larger horses and out of his view. He quickly ran to where the mounts had been hobbled. His donkey was gone.

* * *

He tore off a strip of greasy succulent chicken and stuffed it into his mouth chewing mechanically. He looked down at the half eaten bird in front of him. With a long sweep of his hand he cleared the table, scattering everything onto the floor. He had lost his appetite.

Where were those maladroit incompetents with his Stone? He should never have trusted them with such a vital task. Draig unsheathed his dagger and proceeded to remove the remnants of the chicken from between his teeth as he dwelt on the prospects of the Stone's immense power being infused into him. He was mindful of those cursed words of prophecy. The Stone was meant for Megan. He would have to use his own magic to divert the power to him. Some sort of possession transference spell would be required. He would devise some way.

Draig's dental maintenance and his acquisition designs were interrupted as the head Heinion floated ghostlike in through the rock wall of his cave. It began speaking excitedly in its highly strung staccato voice. "Master Draig, we bring good news. We have secured The Stone. We are much smarter than …"

Its imminent launch into self aggrandizement was cut short abruptly by Draig angrily slamming his dagger into the wooden table.

"Where is my Stone?"

"Err, here, my Lord." The Heinion produced a donkey's ear in its outstretched bony three fingered hand.

"What is this? You incompetent fool. Where is my Stone?"

"Master look harder. You will find it is there, as I have said." It skull like face nodding up and down as it spoke.

Draig took the severed ear in his hand. He immediately noticed the blood covered drawstring and proceeded to draw it forth. A small leather bag appeared dangling on the end of the string. He raised the string up until the bag sat twirling in front of him at eye level. He looked at it and a slow smile parted his lips. He could not contain his excitement any longer.

"Get out," he yelled. The grovelling minion exited through the wall, grinning as it went.

Draig had waited for this moment. He would delay the infusion no longer. He not only wanted the power, he craved it.

Fumbling with the leather tie which held the bag closed, the Zaurlock nervously opened the pouch. He upended its contents into his open palm.

His look of glee quickly changed to one of disappointment. The Stone was not the shining glorious gem that he had imagined. It still had the multi faceted surface, but it was a dull uninspiring black colour.

Legend regarding The Stone had created a picture in his mind of magnificence and splendour, unmatched by any relic or artefact known to man. This was just a piece of worthless rock. Perhaps the incompetents had got it wrong and been given this substitute in place of the genuine article. He rolled the Stone around in his hand as he considered what his next action would be.

Draig carried the Stone in his hand as he went to his small library housed in one of the smaller caves attached to his main dwelling. He opened his hand written copy of The Annals of Magical History to seek more information on The Stone.

After delving deeply into the tome, he discovered that The Stone was indeed this dull black lifeless rock until it was prompted to perform some vital and significant act, which would shape history or change destiny.

Well, he surmised to himself that his need was probably worthy of such an event. He was after all going to dominate the known world. Surely he rated the attention of The Stone's life changing attributes.

Yet he realized that he must first change the meaning of the prophecy to be able to include him in the outworking. The words on the wall had said, that The Stone must be in the hand of the chosen one for it to release the potent power needed to bring about the prophetic promise. If he were to be conveniently joined with her when the power was released, then he could harvest his share. Was this madness? He did not think so. He congratulated himself for his ingenuity and intelligence.

The annals had also said that she must be human in order for the power of The Stone to be released. Drat. He had just performed nothing short of a miracle to morph her into that angry ill tempered panther. In the interests of the greater good for all concerned he should now try to change her back. His record for being able to do that was, at best dubious. Look at Rasita he thought. Such a capable young man locked in the body of a fox. Oh well. But how was he going to control the panther. Last time she had almost torn him apart with those sharp claws of hers. Now, she had some small cause to hate him as well. He was not simply going to have a vicious animal reassembled and brought to him.

He would devise another way he always did.

* * *

She looked at the empty locket again. She was certain that Draig had her Gemma held prisoner. She felt such sadness for her brave helper.

Still faced with the need to contact Sagent Nah she and Rasita discussed their options.

"I could go," said Rasita. "But if I did find him we would still have to travel back to you. It would take time."

"We do not even know where to start. He could be anywhere." Megan sat in the sphinx position her long tail wrapped around her haunches. Her sadness for her Gemma lingered as she thought, when she needed help, how the small being had made things easy for her.

"I am better placed to go. You are far too obvious a target.

You would be the only panther in the kingdom whereas there are foxes everywhere." Rasita's insistence started to make sense.

"What you say is right Rasita. But you have already given so much for me. I cannot ask you to risk your life." Her sense of obligation weighed heavily on her. He had unselfishly given his portion of creature force to save her last time from being permanently morphed into a fox. She loved him for his selflessness. He was to her, a true hero. He was always thinking of others before himself. She determined that she would reward him someday when all this was settled. For now, she would just cherish him as a friend.

At the conclusion of this episode of her life, when she takes up her mantle as the chosen one and the power of The Stone lives and moves within her, she would put things right. Those who had done evil, she would annul, and those who had fostered the cause of good, she would reward. This, she believed was what she was destined to fulfil.

Rasita took her faltering as acquiescence. "I will leave immediately. It may be prudent if I take your locket with me so that Sagent Nah can recognize it, and I am not taken down with an arrow before I can state my case."

"But how can we get it from my neck to yours. These creature paws just don't work the same as human hands," Megan said looking around the cave for anything that might help.

"I can just take it from your throat with my teeth and keep it in my mouth until I get to Sagent Nah." Rasita's ingenuity came shining through again.

He looked at the huge black panther sitting in front of him. She was magnificent, a perfectly formed specimen. Her majestic head held high, not out of arrogance, but stemming out of her regal heart. She was a real princess and the character of the animal really fitted with her personality and behaviour. At least Draig had done that part of his dastardly plan well. What a strange companion for a fox to have, he mused. But then again, these were strange times. He himself was once a man, and she was once a girl, or perhaps now a woman. He actually thought that he was privileged to be part of this momentous occasion, where he gets to work side by side with the chosen one to fix the woes of the world. For him it seemed more than just admiration or his growing devotion. He felt a strange attraction to her that he could not explain.

"Where will you start to look for Nah?" Megan's voice

interrupted his reverie.

"I can start with the Zaurlock's Keep and go from there. If he is not there then perhaps I can overhear some his servants or workers and glean some idea as to where he is." Rasita always seemed to have ideas that were rational.

She raised herself into a sitting position to allow him to use his teeth to pull the locket from her throat. After a few attempts, he backed away from her with a satisfied look on his vulpine face. The broken ends of the golden chain hung from each side of his mouth.

She missed him even before he had gone. She wondered absently how he would have looked when he was a man. She certainly liked his heart which shone through even though he was trapped within the body of this small animal. She remembered vaguely her lessons earlier in the year with the royal tutor when the name Rasita was mentioned. As it was an unusual name it had stuck in her mind. She had asked the tutor about it, and he had explained that the House of Darilus was of the royal blood line which went back many generations, and that the current heir was named Rasita.

Could it be that these two are the same? Is this small fox before her in fact of royal bloodline? When she considered her own plight, the prospect was not so farfetched. She was certainly a royal, and she was certainly a beast.

She risked a rebuff and blurted out her direct enquiry. "Are you of royal blood Rasita?

He looked blankly at her. He had a mouthful of locket and did not want to put it down. A strange thing happened. He projected his answer straight to her mind. The fox language echoed in her thoughts.

"Why do you ask?"

She was at first surprised and then amused. This was yet another extraordinary discovery. They could communicate without talking. It could prove to be a great asset if it worked over distance. She tentatively tried to respond.

"Can you actually hear me Rasita? If you can say 'I love you?'"

An awkward moment passed.

"I love you."

They both made motions of deep laughter as best as their beastly landlords would allow them.

"We can test this out while you are away. I hope that distance is not an issue. This is brilliant."

"I am surprised as well. I have never heard of this before. Do you think that the Holy One is blessing us in this particular way perhaps to show us that He is with us, and that we need to be encouraged to go forward bravely?"

"I choose to believe that what you have said is true. Now go, before I forsake my courage and ask you to stay with me."

Rasita gave an understanding nod and left immediately for the Zaurlock's Keep.

* * *

"They have taken The Stone," the Gimp's face showed that he was deadly serious.

"But only your beast is missing. Where is The Stone? Nah was incredulous. He did not want to believe that he had been fooled so easily by the phantoms.

"As a precaution, I hid it in the donkey's ear." He faced Nah without fear for he had done what he believed to be the best action to protect his charge.

"How did they do it? How did they know?" Nah felt the anger and disappointment rise within him.

"We do not know what powers they possess, they are not from this world. There must have been others working with them." Quan searched for the right words which would relieve them at least a little from the agony of such an easy defeat. He and Nah were supposed to be some of the best warriors in the land. He himself was The Bearer of the Stone. How could he face himself now that he had personally put the princess at further risk through his own neglect?

Nah noticed the look of anxiety and recrimination on his friend's face and it softened his heart toward him. He knew without a shadow of a doubt that Quan would sooner die than fail to fulfil his own high standards of obligation and duty. He reached out to him.

"Quan, do not treat yourself harshly. We are all here to perform our duty, and the best thing to do now is to work out how we are going to recover The Stone, and get it into Megan's hand so that the real power can be released." Nah pondered the possibilities.

Draig had to be behind this. He was the one in the prophecy who had wrongly sought the evil that has pervaded this world.

Those phantoms must have been in his service. Why would they act on their own to acquire The Stone? What was Draig going to do with the relic it was useless to anyone other than Megan, the chosen one.

Unless he thought that by preventing Megan from receiving The Stone, the prophecy could not be fulfilled. A rather foolish notion as he was pitting himself against the will of the Holy One who had already proclaimed the prophecy, setting it in motion. Then there was the second prophecy, also now proclaimed, that his brother had obviously not heard about. It spoke of Megan's victory, which conversely would mean Draig's defeat.

They were still a day's journey from the Eastlands realm. He had little choice now but to return to his Keep and plan from there. He dreaded the duty he had to report to King Henrik his failure to firstly secure his daughter's safety, and secondly, to effectively transport the Stone of Deliverance to her hand. No amount of explanation or reason would excuse him from feeling the full weight of Henrik's wrath. He had quilled the words of both prophecies onto scrolls, which at least held some redemption for him in Henrik's eyes. This was no longer simply an abduction of his daughter by Nah's deranged brother, but she now had been elevated to the position of being the chosen one. This was a war between good and evil with potentially cataclysmic consequences for the earth and Megan was the catalyst.

He still could not fathom where Megan was. He needed to know. The last time she called him she had been morphed into a fox. He had tried to protect her from it happening again, and now he did not even know where she was.

Quan had more of his own regrets and guilt issues to contend with. He vowed that he would not rest until he had recovered The Stone, and placed it safely in a rescued Megan's hand. Only then, would he feel that he had fulfilled his duty to his king, the realm, and now the Holy One. He was a Gimp and his entire race was reputed to be stubbornly loyal and upright.

He could not let them down, but most of all; he could not let himself down. He would be much more diligent when it came to this new threat from the underworld. In his long and contumacious life, he had fought many different races and even beings not human, but he had always been able to better them in the end. This would be no different, he would prevail again.

He sorely regretted losing The Stone. It had been a very personal failure for Quan, one to which he was unaccustomed.

They went searching for Quan's donkey which had not responded to his call. They found it a considerable distance from the campsite. It lay in a ditch bleeding heavily from where the phantoms had cruelly severed its ear. Quan dropped to his knees at his mount's side, speaking soft words of comfort as he did. His loving and loyal nature also extended to his beast. His heart wrenched at the site of the lopsided bloody head. The donkey, hearing his master's voice, tried to get to its feet. Quan rested his hand against the donkey's neck and soothed it back down into a lying position. Nah knelt down beside Quan and said with compassion in his voice.

"Quan let me try my healing chant. It sometimes works on beasts."

The Gimp stood up, and backed away, giving his friend room to perform his magic. The donkey let out a long mournful bray as it sensed its master leaving. Quan looked as if he would burst into tears, as he loved this donkey more than he should.

Sagent Nah laid his hand on the bleeding hole that was once the donkey's ear, and began his healing invocation. Miraculously, the bleeding stopped, and when Nah removed his hand, the hole was healed over leaving a whitish circle of new skin where the wound had been. The donkey got to its feet and immediately went to its master, nuzzling its nose into his chest.

"Well, I have now got the strangest looking donkey in the Eastlands realm." The donkey flicked its good ear in perfect timing, making Quan laugh out loud and causing the others to laugh along with him, giving them a temporary respite to what had been a dreadful day so far.

They broke camp and continued their home journey with their hearts weighed down by the not so encouraging set of events that had transpired.

Chapter 13

King Henrik sat on his throne. He had heard that Sagent Nah had returned and had summoned him immediately. He had not even allowed him the time to settle back into his Keep after a long and difficult journey.

Nah presented himself before the king. He humbly bowed, and when he lifted his head he met the disapproving stare of his monarch.

"Well Chief Zaurlock Nah, where is my daughter?"

Nah would have given anything to be either somewhere else at that moment, or to have been able to give another answer other than the one, which he knew would surely bring the king's wrath down on him.

He had enjoyed a long and successful tenure as Chief Court Zaurlock and as advisor to the king prior to that, but he could not call upon any of that, to make his admission of failure any less distressing and painful for his king. He had no choice, but to tell him the bad news, and to rely upon Henrik's fairness and mercy.

"My lord, forgive me I have failed you." Nah almost chocked on the words, as the gravity of what he had just said dawned on him afresh. He stammered, as he continued his confession. "My king, you charged me with the responsibility to rescue your daughter, and to find means to overcome and defeat the treasonous abductor Draig. I have not found your daughter, nor have I secured as yet, a way to defeat Draig."

Nah knew instinctively that he should now be silent. To launch into a litany of excuses, and reasons for the failure, would only ignite Henrik's wrath even more. He waited in silence for Henrik to speak.

Henrik inhaled deeply, and breathed out a long breath through his nose, before speaking in a grave tone.

"I have known you Nah for many years. In that time you have proven your allegiance and loyalty to the realm. It is for that reason that I chose you to undertake this mission. I believe that you have tried your best to do my bidding, and I do not hold you accountable for this initial failing. What I am now interested in, is the next step you are going to take to find my daughter. Do you have any idea where she is being held?" Henrik sat back in his throne grasping his chin with his right hand while placing his elbow on the armrest.

"My king, I thank you sincerely for your gracious response to my failing, and your continuing belief in me. My latest intelligence tells me the whereabouts of Draig. He has moved his camp to the Hajus Woods. If we can find him, we can find Megan. My spies have told me that part of Draig's mountain cave was demolished; they are guessing that it was a result of some magical altercation. They also found his dead HuverWort on the floor of the cave, and a large empty gilded cage."

Henrik stood to his feet signalling to the commander of his army as he rose. "Take a contingent of your best men and go to the Hajus Woods immediately. Apprehend the abductor Zaurlock Draig and bring him here to me. Use whatever force you need."

"My king, if I may interject." Nah took an extreme risk speaking at this particular time.

"Yes, quickly Nah speak now."

"If Draig is holding Megan, and we send in your soldiers Draig, in his madness may choose to harm her before we can stop him. Please allow me another chance to complete what you have asked me to do."

The king raised a hand halting the departure of the commander, and issued to him this command. "Wait on my order. Keep your men in readiness to leave at short notice."

Henrik saw the logic in Nah's counsel. He needed level heads around him at this time, as he was far too emotionally involved to make detached decisions. When he thought about it, apart from Megan, he trusted Nah more than anyone else in the Eastlands realm.

"You have your chance Nah, but do not fail me again. I want your full report of what happened on your quest to Alabasteil, and your strategy to remedy this situation by noon tomorrow."

The king rose and walked out of the throne room, signalling to all that conversation had ended.

* * *

Gemma felt as though she was sagging under the weight of loss and disappointment. Her colour had faded to a light grey, reflecting her dour mood. She missed her mistress Megan. Her entire existence was dedicated to serving the princess. She also felt that she had failed Megan, in that she had not made it to Sagent Nah, when Megan needed him so badly.

Whatever magical constraint Draig had placed on her was too strong for her to break. She was trapped. She had tried expanding herself to twice the size to break the aura cage, but it only hurt her to do so, and she abandoned the idea. She could not stay here when her princess needed her. She flopped back against the aura and wept.

"Do not waste your tears on someone who will soon be gone."

Draig waved his hand, and the aura cage moved from its position in the corner of the cave ceiling to where he was seated. He studied the Halopod closely with his inky eyes as it floated just in front of his face. He could use this little creation. His brother was not as backward as he first thought. His work was truly superb. He used his magic to delve further into the structure and make up of his little captive. Well done Nah. He grudgingly said in his mind, as he saw just how the little being functioned. This was even better than his HuverWort. The thought of his dead minion gave him an instant of regret, before he moved on; thinking that he now had a very good replacement. He just needed to change the way this sentimental little imp thought. It needed some toughening up, but he could see real potential in it. He had remembered training the HuverWort. It had been reasonably easy with the help of his Searing Twitch. It would also provide him with some entertainment. It was becoming rather boring around the cave since Megan had escaped. His expression changed to one of wickedness as he dwelt on the prospect.

Gemma peered at the Zaurlock through the hazy shimmer of the aura cage. She could see by the changing expressions on his face that he was planning something, and that she was the subject.

"I am going to train you little imp to be my servant. I like the way you are so devoted to Megan, but that has to end. You would do well to change your allegiance to me, because the pain from this … will be used to help you decide." He produced from under his robes the Searing Twitch. He released a quick charge from the end of the rod, sending a spiralling tendril of concentrated potential pain crackling into the air. It evaporated, leaving the acrid smell of burnt flesh lingering.

The Halopod drew back in fear. She had heard Megan's screams of agony coming through the walls of the locket as Draig had tortured her. She knew what the Twitch was capable of doing. In her mind she devised a plan. There was no need for her to endure pain. She was unsure if her small frame could handle the venomous piercings of the Twitch.

She was no good to Megan if she was dead or worse if she had truly given herself over to Draig, and was working against her mistress.

She planned to convince Draig that she had truly gone over to his side. That in itself would produce enough pain, both physical and emotional, but it was by far the best alternative.

She could achieve much more for Megan's cause if she was privy to Draig's devious machinations. Her decision made, she began her work immediately on her new covert role.

"Please do not use that thing on me!" She feigned a look of terror on her small face. It was not hard to do as she really did feel very afraid. Her real sense of fear added credence to her ruse.

"I was there when you used it on Megan. I heard her screams. Please, I beg you, do not hurt me. I will do anything you ask. Master Draig."

He looked searchingly and sceptically deep into her wavering eyes. His piercing intense glare sought any morsels of untruth.

"That seems a little too easy." He touched the aura cage with his Twitch. She wailed. Her small voice rang out piercingly, causing an echo to resound off the impervious cave walls.

"No, stop please. I said that I would serve you. I do not want any more pain Master Draig." She collapsed on to the cage floor exhausted from just one touch of the dreadful Twitch.

Draig was still not convinced that she had capitulated so quickly. Her innate nature was constructed in such a way that she was totally loyal and committed to her charge. He liked the undying devotion aspect, but was suspicious that she could shift her allegiance so easily to him. We shall see he mused absently to himself. Perhaps a little more pain would purify her intentions.

He looked at the now unconscious Halopod lying on the cage floor, and decided that she looked too pure and holy for his liking. He would change that as well. It would never do for him to have one of his minions looking so saintly and pure. But before that this little imp may make excellent bait for the sentimental princess.

He shook the aura roughly with his hand, but she did not stir. Later he thought. His surveillance web sounded a movement vibration. Somebody was leaving his woods.

Draig saw the rear end of a fox just passing through the outer bounds of his web.

"Let him go," he said aloud to nobody but himself. "I have no need for him. He is permanently morphed, and presents no real threat to me."

He still felt soreness in his lower leg where that vulpine nuisance had so callously bitten him. Keep that in mind, he thought. All will be repaid once he gains full control. He will be unstoppable. His hand went to the folds of his robe. Feeling The Stone, he rotated it in his bony hand.

He could hardly wait.

* * *

Rasita had run through most of the night, as he reasoned that he would be seen less that way. As he loped along, he thought about Megan. She was now a woman and no longer a girl. What was that sensation he had felt when she asked him to say the words 'I love you'? Yes it was true, if he had to admit it, he did love her, but as a princess, yet, there was something more. His heart leapt within him when he thought of her. It was as if his whole body floated above the ground when he was in her presence. It was anything but an unpleasant feeling, it was just one he had never experienced before. Was it love? Real romantic love?

He immediately chided himself for his foolishness. He must remember who, or more to the point what, he was. He was a fox. A lowly animal. He had no business daydreaming about a human, let alone a princess of royal blood. It also reminded him of his previous commitment, when he had wanted so badly to be Draig's apprentice and his father had flatly refused his request. His father did not have the gift, and could not understand his attraction to alphawizardry. In the end, Rasita had to relinquish his birthright in order to pursue his calling.

Now, he was without even that. Trapped forever in his vulpine body he accepted his lot, and cleared his mind of any further thoughts of love. He concentrated his mental efforts on the task ahead.

The gold chains hanging from either side of his mouth bobbed and bounced against his neck and lips, reminding him of his mission. He had to find Nah. He would know what to do.

Rasita had to be careful that he was not the victim of some overzealous hunters who could inadvertently prevent him from completing his mission by killing him, just for the sport of it.

The dawn was just breaking as he approached Nah's Keep. He slowed his pace to a walk using his sensitive nose to check the wind for scents of possible friend or foe. His nose picked up the pungent scent of a donkey. He approached an outdoor open fenced enclosure abutting the Keep stables. It had the appearance of an exercise yard for the horses. Standing near the wooden rail closest to him was a strange looking donkey. It had only one ear. Not one to scoff, Rasita wondered how such a misfortune could have come about.

He suddenly thought of something outlandish to try. Could he possibly project his thoughts to this donkey? Nothing ventured, nothing gained, and he proceeded to try.

"I am looking for Sagent Nah the white Zaurlock."

He waited, not really expecting a reply.

"I know of him."

Rasita jolted backwards, almost hitting his head against the tree around which he had been peeking.

"Why are you so surprised that I can hear you fox?" The donkey stuck his lopsided head out through the gap between the rails.

"*I, well, I,*" stammered the fox, "*I did not really expect that you would answer me.*"

"*I am no ordinary donkey. I belong to Quan the Gimp. He is 'The Bearer of The Stone,'*" the animal proudly announced, as if Rasita was to immediately appreciate what that entailed.

"*Would that be the Stone of Deliverance?*"

It was now the donkey's turn to be surprised. It recovered its stoicism quickly and replied. "*Why, yes fox. How did you come by this knowledge?*"

"*Enough of the question jousting donkey, I need to see Sagent Nah urgently. Mention Princess Megan and her locket and he will understand. I know that you are smart. Can you contact him?*"

The donkey seemed satisfied that this fox did not have evil intentions, so he turned his head toward the Keep and let out a long mournful bray.

In a very short time Quan the Gimp appeared. Rasita slipped back in behind the tree and waited, not completely confident that he had done the right thing trusting the donkey.

Quan went immediately to the donkey's side. "*What is it my lookout. What have you seen?*"

Rasita then witnessed an almost familiar communication happen between the man and his beast. It was in a language that he did not understand, but he got the idea that what was being said was helpful.

"*A fox wants to see Nah urgently. He looks genuine. He said to mention Megan and some locket of hers.*"

Quan went immediately indoors. A minute later Sagent Nah appeared, looking searchingly toward the line of trees at the forest edge.

He spoke in Eastlander tongue, "Do not be frightened Rasita, if it is you. I remember you. Come out, we have no time to waste."

Rasita took the chance and padded his way from behind the tree and into the morning light. He walked toward Nah and as he approached him, Nah noticed the gold chain hanging from the fox's mouth. When he reached Nah's knees the Zaurlock placed his open palm under Rasita's mouth. The locket dropped into his hand. Nah recognized it as Megan's.

"Come Rasita, we have much to do before noon today we must stand before the king and show him how we intend to save his daughter."

They all stepped back into the door of the Keep kitchen, leaving Quan's donkey to his own inimitable company.

* * *

Noon came all too soon for Nah and Rasita. They, along with Quan had spent all of their time preparing their strategy for Megan's rescue plan.

They were mindful of the time as King Henrik was one for punctuality.

The three entered the king's court, one fraction before the gong sounded heralding the entrance of the king himself.

Their hearing had obviously been shifted to first place. They were shuffled forward with much murmuring from the assembly about the fox's presence in court.

The king sat eyeing the fox with knitted brows. The assembly also seated themselves with minimal noise. The king motioned to Nah to begin.

"Your Majesty, you have charged me with the task of rescuing your daughter …"

The king, in uncustomary short manner slammed his fist on the arm rest of his throne. "Get on with it Nah. What have you found out?"

The white Zaurlock was taken aback at the king's outburst. He quickly collected himself and stated succinctly his findings.

"I present to you, and the court, Lord Rasita Darilus." Nah made a sweeping gesture toward the fox.

The murmurs of disbelief rose from the assembly.

"Is this some sort of jest?" The king looked around the court for someone to restore sanity.

"Allow me to explain your Majesty. This fox was once Rasita Darilus. He is of the royal bloodline. He was morphed in similar fashion to your daughter by Draig in his insanity. Rasita has been with Megan, and knows where to find her."

"At last some progress." Henrik breathed in a long breath. "Continue."

Nah did not want to say his next statement, but he was committed to presenting a full and frank report to his king. "We have discovered that Princess Megan has been morphed yet again; this time into a black panther."

A hush came over the people as they waited for king Henrik

to react to this terrible news.

He bowed his head and placed his hand over his eyes. He gradually raised his head again. His hand sliding to his chin, as his eyes opened once more. After a long moment he spoke.

"Can she be brought back again as she was last time?" Hopefulness reflected in his sombre tone.

"We have other good news that may provide the answer to your question. There have been two prophecies proclaimed. Both of which refer to the princess as the chosen one. This gives us the confidence that the Holy One is indeed with Megan, and that He will deliver her for His purpose. We believe that she will be restored to her human form to take up her mantle as the chosen one." He stopped to allow the king to comment. When he did not respond Nah continued.

"I have Megan's necklace and locket brought to me by Rasita the fox." He nodded a tacit apology at Rasita for referring to him as a fox. He produced the necklace and handed it to the king.

Henrik caressed it fondly in his large hand as if it was actually his precious Megan. The tears brimmed up in his eyes but did not fall to his cheeks. He could not let his people see him in weakness. The many years of public life stood by him.

The Chief Court Zaurlock continued his discourse.

"Unfortunately, the shroud between the earth the deep earth has been rent, and minions from the underworld have pervaded our realm. We were confronted by them on our journey, and we lost possession of The Stone of Deliverance."

Henrik's face was unreadable, but his eyes did not leave Nah.

"Draig is back in the Hajus Woods. We believe that he has The Stone, but it is useless in his hands. He is not the chosen one. He is the one who seeks evil wrongly, as spoken about in the first prophecy."

Nah paused then delivered more of his report.

"We have diligently scribed the words of the two prophecies which have been proclaimed. We will submit them to the court."

He started to speak further when Quan, who was standing beside him, suddenly raised his hands to the heavens. His eyes took on that glazed distant look, and he again was surrounded by the holy light that they had witnessed last time he prophesied. He began to speak words of prophecy in front of the multitude of witnesses.

"This is the third prophecy which I the Holy One proclaim this day. My innocent, My chosen one, will be returned to the embrace of her forebear. The Day of Drawing is coming when My best will be made to be together to defend right on the Plains of Rescuse. Thereafter, on the Day of Deliverance those who seek and persist in wrong will be banished into the pit. Thence the Day of Restoration will surely follow and true love will blossom like the fruit tree in season."

Quan collapsed onto the floor and lay still. The look of exhaustion from the concentration of effort was evidenced on his face.

"My Liege, it seems that we now have three prophesies to submit. I will provide a full report to you of all events to date."

Henrik rose to his feet. "Sagent Nah, take my soldiers and bring Megan back to me. We now have a holy mandate, so you can go with confidence. May the Holy One be with you."

Chapter 14

Megan stretched her long sleek ebony body. She arched her back in the stretch; her front paws extended out in front of her as her sinewy torso almost touched the ground. She watched, as the sharp claws protruded out of her pads and then disappeared again as she shifted back into an upright stance. The strong muscles and tendons flexed and rippled with the movement. She was getting accustomed to being a lithe, powerful panther.

Venturing outside the cave she sniffed the morning air. Many different scents filled her sensitive nostrils. She had not mastered the skill of identifying each as yet, but she was noticing the same ones recurring, and she could almost recognize some as distinct from others.

She went over to the rivulet and before drinking, she looked at the reflection of herself in the pond of still water. Her jet black head was streamlined to perfection. Her emerald green eyes shone fiercely amid the dark background. She bared her fangs peeling back her whiskered lips in a mock snarl just to see how it looked. The image startled her. She could look very scary if the occasion arose. Letting her lips cover her fangs again she peered at the beastly splendour before her. She almost imagined Gemma floating innocently over her shoulder. What had happened to her little servant? She dreaded the thought of harm befalling the tiny being and pushed it from her mind.

She dropped down and drank deeply, lapping the cool water into her mouth. Even that was different for her. It somehow made the water taste better than just drinking it straight down. Things were certainly different in so many ways. She had experienced events in her short life that should never occur in the life of a normal young girl.

Finishing her water she sunned herself, sitting just outside the cave mouth. Even the Hajus Woods had allowed a warm stream of sunshine to break through the dark canopy, and grace her with its soothing heat this morning. Should she take that as a positive sign that things were getting better. She decided that she would.

A plethora of thoughts robbed her of the simple pleasure of the warm sun on her back. She wondered if Rasita had made it to Nah's Keep safely. He was becoming something special to her she decided. Her thoughts of him were changing. She surmised that she was no longer a ten year old. She would never have had these thoughts at that age. She must have retained in her mind the age leap to eighteen or nineteen that Draig had orchestrated in his madness.

She remembered their accidental venture into projected thoughts. How bizarre it was that she could now project her thoughts in a language that she was unsure whether it was Eastlander tongue, fox or panther, and be able to hear back a response in similar fashion from another animal. Truly bizarre.

Had she subconsciously prompted Rasita to say the words 'I love you' just to see his reaction to her? Probably, she tried to answer herself honestly. There was definitely an attraction there that she did not fully understand.

Looking from the outside in, this would seem like madness. A female black panther has romantic thoughts about a male fox? Both are really humans. It would not even rate as suitable material for a drunken tale at the tavern.

She brought her mind back to Nah. She must assume that Rasita somehow has alerted him to her whereabouts, and that he would soon be here to escort her back to the palace. How could she face her father in this form? Hopefully, Nah would have explained things. Would he still love her if she could not be changed back? She purposely took hold of her racing thoughts. She must keep the words of the prophecy top of her mind. She was the chosen one. The Holy One was with her. Things would work out right in the end.

She breathed in a long deep breath and sighed resolutely.

She had witnessed firsthand the power of the Words to deliver her from bondage. Had they not smashed down the walls of Draig's cavern, and opened the way for her to escape? She filled herself with the comfort of those events.

She would be brave and strong.

* * *

"Can I watch?" the screechy voice of the head Heinion pleaded to his master for permission to sit in on the training of the Halopod.

Draig turned deliberately from his work to face the fidgeting swaying minion. His top lip curled in a lopsided beguiling slur, showing some yellowed teeth in the gap. He held the smouldering hot Searing Twitch in his hand.

He resented the interruption just when he was about to start his entertainment.

"Why yes, come over here and I will give you a closer look at how it works." Draig's dry lips parted in a mock welcoming smile, as he consoled himself that this might prove to be a good entrée to the main event. The fool needed some sharpening up.

The hapless fiend wafted over to where Draig had the Halopod sitting on his work bench in front of him.

As it came within striking distance of the Twitch, Draig noticed the single shrivelled nipple which protruded like a dried raison from the centre of its chest. Ideal, he thought extending the Twitch to touch the prune like protuberance.

The legless Heinion launched itself backwards grabbing for the wounded body part, as it yowled horrendously in pain. It retreated at speed through the solid rock wall, not looking back in its haste.

"Fool." Draig smiled and shook his head in disbelief at the naivety of the Heinion.

Gemma stiffened at the sound of the Heinion screaming. She was still resolute in her plan to be Megan's covert helper. She knew that she was inherently strong which did not show in her soft personality and appearance. She hoped that she could endure what was to come. She braced herself and fixed her mind on Megan.

"What is my first assignment for you, Master Draig?" Gemma began again her strategy to convince him that she was now his loyal servant.

"Keen are we?" He smirked and then pursed his lips in obvious doubt regarding her sincerity. "We shall see. First things first."

He studied her making her feel conspicuous. "We need to roughen up your appearance somewhat."

He held his chin as if considering his choices. "Ah yes that should suffice." He extended his index finger and in a drawing motion, inscribed the air in front of him.

She felt as if her features were being altered in some way. Her face felt tighter and she could see a set of newly acquired eyebrows descending into her line of vision. She dreaded the thought of what he was creating.

"There, much more appropriate for one of my minions." He sat back admiring his handiwork.

"What have you done to me?" asked the Halopod, feeling suddenly demoralized.

"Never you mind little imp. Just remember who owns you now. I can do whatever I like and you must choose to be happy with it." He flicked his hand upwards and the aura cage floated back up to the cave ceiling.

Draig had more important things to do. His little imp's training could wait.

He produced The Stone from under his robes and studied the bauble carefully. It began to shimmer with light as the power from its core increased in intensity.

"Ah," exclaimed the delighted Zaurlock. "It's about time we had some action."

As the intensity of light and power increased so did the heat.

Draig could not hold The Stone any longer in his hand. It burned his palm and it was as if it was denying his right to hold it. He licked his burned hand to try to sooth the hurting.

The Stone fell to the bench where it continued to increase its sanctified glow.

It shone with every rainbow colour imaginable, shooting shafts of light fanning out into the dark interior of the cave. Out of its centre came a flow of Words undulating forth toward the rock surface of the cave wall.

"Not again," Draig cursed in a whiney voice.

The last time this happened his whole place was all but demolished.

The Words of the second and third prophecies etched themselves into the hard rock wall.

Draig shadowed his eyes with his hand not wanting to read them.

They filled the space on the wall from top to bottom, declaring their warning to those which it applied.

The Zaurlock dropped his hand and looked fearfully at the writing, as a voice deeply resonant and awesome, sounded forth the Words.

Draig went to cover his ears with his hands, but was prevented from doing so by an unknown force, which he was powerless against.

"This is the second prophecy that I the Holy One speak and proclaim this day. This Stone carries with it my blessing. My innocent waits on the Plain of Rescuse beyond the Valley of Bones. Adversity rises and resists my will but it will wane for The Stone shall be united with my innocent and the battle is won in the worldly realm.

"This is the third prophecy which I the Holy One proclaim this day. My innocent, My chosen one will be returned to the embrace of her forebear. The Day of Drawing is coming when My best will be made to be together to defend right on the Plains of Rescuse. Thereafter on the Day of Deliverance those who seek and persist in wrong will be banished into the pit. Thence the Day of Restoration will surely follow and true love will blossom like the fruit tree in season."

The power seemed to abate but the feeling of dread haunted the black Zaurlock. The words remained written into the wall.

He tried to work out his part in the prophecy. Was he the chosen one? He could be. No, even he thought that the possibility was rather remote. It referred to a female. It must be Megan.

It reinforced in him his previous conclusion that he had to regain control of her. He had to be there when she released the power of The Stone so that he could siphon off his share. She would not do it willingly; she had to be persuaded to see it his way.

He looked deviously up at the Halopod. She would play a part in this. He would use the little imp to lure her to his cave, and once he had her again in his power, he would influence her to include him in the blessing.

As he looked away Gemma smiled secretly to herself. She would certainly play her part in this.

* * *

The soldiers moved out in formation through the palace gates. Sagent Nah, mounted on his grey warhorse headed up the contingent. Quan sat his donkey and rode just behind Nah. All were in full battle dress and regalia displaying the insignia of the Eastlands realm on their shields. The sound of weaponry jingled in unison with the horses tack as they trotted along. Fluttering in the wind ensigns, atop of the long staffs issued their challenge. A fortified cage on a low wagon drawn by four strong working horses, followed up at the rear.

Quan's lop sided; one eared donkey looked out of place in the presence of the magnificent battle hardened steeds. It did not however seem intimidated by their presence.

Rasita trotted silently along beside the leaders, his long tail a plume behind him.

Nah was in good spirits as they were finally going to bring Megan home. The fact that she was a panther did not help matters, but at least they had her in spirit. He secretly hoped that the outworking of the prophecy would be the answer to her being restored. The third prophecy spoke about a day of restoration. Surely the chosen one would warrant special attention on that day. His confidence was high. After all the setbacks, he now had a royal, and a spiritual mandate to do what he had been struggling to achieve before.

He looked across at Quan. He appeared so awkward and unimposing sitting on his disfigured donkey. Yet the Holy One had chosen him to deliver all three of the prophecies. He was in his own way truly remarkable. It was an honour to know him. Quan still had not gotten over losing The Stone, so this was for him, a personal quest to regain his worth in his own eyes. He was an honourable person and Nah could not but feel warm toward him.

Draig was already banished from the realm. He was officially an outlaw. Nah's commission was not to apprehend him particularly, but if he resisted, then he would use all the physical force of the king's own palace guard and all of his and Quan's combined magical power, to bring his brother to heel. He had long since abandoned ideals of kinship with Draig. He had overstepped so many boundaries that Nah was inured to any sentimentality whatsoever.

The Hajus Woods was only a short ride from the palace, so

he would not have to wait long to begin his corrective work. They could access the Woods via an old lumber road which led almost directly to the centre, where Rasita had said Megan's cave was situated.

Rasita had taken the lead to direct the others to Megan. No doubt Draig would know ahead of time of their arrival in his haunt. It did not matter, from what Rasita had said Megan was not his prisoner, and she had intimidated him on their last encounter as she was now a fierce opponent. Draig had created his own nemeses in morphing Megan into a ferocious beast that had a lasting grudge against him. From what Nah knew of his brother, he would now be spending his time scheming rather than confronting Megan.

They reached the outer tree line of the Hajus Woods. Nah raised his hand and brought the soldiers to a halt. To ensure that he got Megan out successfully, he thought that he would send Rasita ahead to go directly to Megan and alert her of their intentions, while they distracted Draig. Rasita agreed, and after giving them clear directions as to the whereabouts of Draig's cave, he headed off immediately into the woods to find his special friend.

* * *

Draig felt the vibrations as the fox disturbed his web. He observed him coming back at quite a fast pace. He was about to send something toward him to halt his progress significantly, when he felt a much more urgent need for his attention. A large number of soldiers were storming into the woods, and they were heading his way. He was not afraid of mere human warriors, but he had to decide, and decide quickly whether he wanted a confrontation right now or not.

Were they coming for him, surely they would not be so foolish. He had decided long ago that when he made his choice to go to the other side, that he would not do so unless he had the magical firepower to defend himself if this situation arose. He could obliterate them he was sure. But he also observed his brother with that Gimp tagging along. They could make things more interesting. He was not unaware of their combined power, and if he was distracted by them, he could be attacked physically by any of the hundreds of soldiers that were heading aggressively in his direction.

They could have their day of this and their day of that, he would have his 'Day of Victory,' but it was not going to be today. After all, he had The Stone and they did not. He could not risk losing it in some minor skirmish. He would reserve his strength for the main event.

Now was not the time for him to seek his revenge. He could wait. A smart leader knows when to choose his time of battle. A hasty retreat was the wisest move. He collected his few essentials like his spell books, the Halopod, the Twitch and of course The Stone, and he headed unobtrusively back to his cave at Mount Isnar.

* * *

Rasita loped silently and quickly along the wide cleared roadway through the woods heading for the cave where Megan should be waiting for him. His mouth spread in his vulpine grin as he signalled ahead by using their newly found thought projection ability.

"Megan, I am almost to the cave. We come with many soldiers. We are going home."

The panther was sitting in the sphinx position with her eyes closed resting. She had nothing more to do than just wait, so she took advantage of the lull by enjoying the time in a drowsy half sleep.

The words dropped into her consciousness and brought her to her feet in an instant. She was immediately alert and fully awake. She replied enthusiastically.

"Rasita I'm so glad that you made it safely. I've missed you."

Within a short space of time Rasita came bounding through the cave opening. They rushed at each other embracing in their awkward animal way. It did not matter the warmth that emanated from each of their hearts was what really made the reunion feel absolutely amazing for them. They were both a little shocked at the depth of feeling that was immediately evident and continued unabated.

Feeling duly embarrassed, they parted, and Megan introduced another line of thought to alleviate the self consciousness they both felt.

"Does my father know that I am like this?" she gave herself a sweeping gaze.

"Yes, he has been told."

"So how did he react?"

"He seemed calm." Rasita spoke less rather than more, as he was not completely sure that her father would understand. He himself had not had good past experiences with fathers and difficult situations.

Megan had to admit that she was anything but calm when she thought about seeing her father. How would they greet each other? He could not speak panther language or even fox language for that matter. They could not even hug each other. The safety of her father's embrace now seemed like such a foolish notion. Her sombre mood was lifted as she pictured him wrapping his arms around a large ferocious black beast to console it. She attempted to laugh out aloud.

"What?" Rasita had been watching her facial expressions as she spun the wheels of her mind, thinking her usual torrent of thoughts, and then she just burst out in what looked like a laugh. Her feline face was contorted with tightly closed eyes and her mouth stretched back in a sort of smile. A series of sneeze like sounds issued forth from her, as she nodded her head up and down. He was not exactly sure he really wanted to know what was happening.

She quickly related to him her reason for the theatrics, causing him also to give his best impression of a laugh.

They really needed to get out of these animal bodies and return to some normal behaviour patterns.

There brief caper into mirth was quickly ended when they heard the sound of horses coming from outside the cave.

"Rasita! Megan!" Nah hailed them as he drew his mount up to the cave entrance. His horse shifted nervously as it picked up the scent of the panther. Shaking its large head about and clawing the ground with its hoof.

Nah dismounted and passed his reins to Quan. He walked into the cave and stood at the entrance. His tall silhouette blocked the light and darkened the interior of the cave a little more.

He waited for a short moment while his eyes adjusted to the dimness before seeing clearly the scene before him. A large black panther sat on its haunches looking directly at him. His first reaction was one of fear. The animal was huge. Panthers were extremely rare in the Eastlands realm. He had to tell himself that this panther was actually Megan, a beautiful little princess and not a ferocious beast ready to pounce on him and devour him. It helped to relieve his initial reaction as he knew that she had been morphed into a panther. It was just the reality of actually seeing her that took some adjustment. Rasita helped by moving over and sitting between her front legs. His head fitted neatly under her deep chest. She put her regal head down and licked his face affectionately.

"Megan?" was all he could get out.

She reverted to fox language which she knew from the last time, that he could understand.

"Sagent Nah, you cannot imagine how pleased I am to see you."

It took him a while to reconcile the response with the speaker. Before him was a panther speaking fox language who was not really a panther but a ten year old princess. Yet she sounded older and more mature. He had seen a great many odd things in his long and interesting life but this was quite uncanny.

He dignified the situation as best as he could manage by acting toward her in a normal fashion.

"I am also very pleased to finally find you, and that you are safe." He was still a little awkward but he was gradually becoming accustomed to the fierce emerald green eyes that looked so intently at him.

"Let us not waste any more time in this dark wood. I have bought transport for you Megan. Come." He turned from the cave opening and went outside.

Megan and Rasita followed. Megan appeared first padding regally into the sunlight. At the sight of her both man and beast reacted tensely and drew back in fear. The horses jostled and reared in an attempt to withdraw all at once. Only Quan's donkey held firm and did not react. The soldiers and their mounts had backed off some way down the road and the horses seemed to settle down with the safety the distance created.

"Bring that wagon forward." Nah gave his order to two of the soldiers sitting on the front of what looked to Megan like a jail on wheels.

The four heavily built horses took up the strain and the wagon lurched forward. The quad of large working stock horses did not seem as nervous in the presence of the panther as did their more spirited cousins.

Megan was perplexed at the sight of the boarded cage. Her recent torturous experience in Draig's cage left her with a natural abhorrence for being locked up. She would have preferred to have walked back to the palace.

"What is this?" she questioned Nah turning to face him squarely.

Nah sensing her reluctance and feeling her rising anger, tried to placate her.

"Your father thought that for your protection, this would be the best way for you to travel. There are many who would not understand who you are, and may seek to harm you. Then there are those who know exactly who you are, and would have perhaps more reason to cause you harm. It is the wisest thing to do."

Megan moved over closer to the wagon and peered into the inner darkness of the enclosed cage. She did not want to enter, but saw the sense in what Nah had said. Her father was as usual right in his thinking and he was only looking out for her safety. She padded her way up the short ramp and entered the cage.

She shuddered as the heavy wooden doors were closed and secured behind her. She peered at the throng of soldiers down the roadway through the thin eye slots cut into the walls of the cage. She fought against the feeling of entrapment in her gut. She noticed Rasita looking up at her from the dusty road. It would not be long she told herself and she would be free again. She secretly hoped that her freedom would also involve release from this beastly cloak. The wagon rocked and swayed as it moved off sluggishly in the direction of the palace.

* * *

The procession arrived back at the palace moving in orderly succession over the moat bridge, and in through the entrance to the palace forecourt. She felt a sense of safety as her wagon passed through the big wrought iron gates. The palace had represented for her a place of security for all of her short life. Now she was back, albeit not in the same form, but she was back.

Her homecoming was not the gala event that a princess would usually expect. It was more like a group of soldiers returning from war with a captive in tow. They milled into the main court and began dispersing and unhitching their horses, and doing all those mundane things that required their immediate attention. Megan observed them through the eye slots and it gave her some sense of comfort seeing ordinary familiar things occurring. She welcomed the break from all the excitement of late which had literally turned her life inside out.

The doors to her cage were opened at last. The fresh air gushed in and she breathed it in lifting her head and drawing it in through her nose.

She walked down the short ramp looking both ways as she did. The townsfolk had turned out to see what was happening when they saw the contingent of the king's guards returning. She noticed the looks of fear cast at her way from people within the crowd. She reasoned that they had probably never seen a black panther before and she ignored them.

Nah led her through a series of secret back passageways, which led to the king's private rooms. She had known of these, and had explored them frequently in her play time. They always seemed so dark when she had seen them before, but now they seemed so much brighter. She assumed that it was because she now viewed them through her panther eyes which were much more sensitive than her human ones.

She knew where they were headed. She and her father had spent many hours there together. He always took her there when he wanted to share with her, something special or serious. He had taken her there when he had to tell her about her mother. She chocked up afresh at the memory. She still had not gotten over her mother's passing. She pondered as they walked why was it that she had to grow up so quickly and why she could not just remain a little girl without the complications of life forcing her to mature before her time.

They entered the room via a sliding secret door disguised as a book shelf. Her father sat on his usual chair facing her as she entered. She looked around at the familiar surroundings and it gave her immediate comfort. The empty chair across from him was where she would sit when they were here together. Obviously she could not sit there this time. She sat down on her haunches beside it on the floor. She noticed her locket and chain sitting on the sideboard beside her father's chair.

Nah came in behind her and stood to one side of the doorway. He would usually be dismissed at this point but without him they could not communicate. Megan looked straight into her father's eyes. The look on his face was not what she had expected from a father being reunited with his lost daughter. His brows were knitted, and he looked troubled, and his eyes flickered from side to side in a nervous tic. It was so unlike him.

She tried to understand what he was experiencing. His only daughter was now a black panther. She just wanted to hug him, and for him to hug her and tell her that everything was going to be alright, but that was clearly not going to happen immediately. She looked for support to Sagent Nah.

He sensed the awkwardness and volunteered a suggestion.

"Majesty, is there something that you want to say to Megan? Just ask her, and I can translate her responses back to you."

The king struggled with the request. He was never without his composure, or a suitable answer. This time he was completely dumbfounded. He looked distressed at his inability to respond.

Megan had never seen him this way, and it hurt her to see him like this. She wanted to reach out to him, but could not. She said to Nah.

"Tell my father that I love him … and that everything will be alright."

Nah translated her message to her father.

He almost broke down when he heard the words. He spread his hands toward her in a gesture of bewilderment.

She did not know what to do next. Confusion framed his face, and a look of almost abhorrence for her streamed from his eyes.

"Take it away from me," he yelled as he turned his face away from her. His wrenching tone tore at her heart.

She looked to Nah for support. His eyes acknowledging her distress at her father's lashing response. She stood, and just looked at her father. She was broken-hearted.

"Come Megan. Leave your father to work through his shock," Nah said softly to her in fox language.

If it were possible for a panther to appear sad then Megan was a good example. She dropped her head and hunched her shoulders, as if the barb was actually piercing her physical heart. Her tail sagged listlessly between her legs, and she turned slowly and slinked out of the room, back into the semi darkness of the passageway. Her mood and demeanour matched the dark atmosphere around her.

She walked down the passageway with Nah at her side. She wished Rasita were there. More than anyone, he would understand what she felt right now. How could her own father reject her like that? It meant so much to her. She felt that her whole world was crashing down around her.

She silently prayed to the Holy One for strength and comfort.

Chapter 15

Draig hated the mess that his cave had become. He could have performed some mundane magical clean up repair work, but he was very much unmotivated. He would have tolerate it. Even that great hole in the wall was letting in some much needed fresh air.

He was more interested in training his new recruit. The Halopod now looked like one of his. He had made her look mean. He now had to match her personality with her looks.

When he had arrived, he had hastily placed her in the corner of the ceiling until he was ready to commence her training.

He gained a sense of pleasure in being able to recreate a personality, especially in one that had belonged to Megan.

He drew her down from the ceiling. She was still encased in her aura cage. He had not completed his modifications as yet. She still needed appendages. She would be of more use to him if she could carry things around. His real reason for the addition of arms was to have somewhere to be able to attach his gossamer dragline to her so that he could test her loyalty without her escaping when he was not looking. If she tried without permission to vacate the mountain and return to her old mistress, she would reach the extent of the dragline and be stopped in a painful jarring fashion. A little like hitting an invisible rock wall. As much as he liked using the Searing Twitch, he had noticed that she had almost faded away last time he had only touched the aura cage. Best train her some other way. He did not have a fabulous record with his little messenger minions. The dead HuverWort was his case in point.

He was unaware that someone was listening in on his thoughts. Even when Draig had delved into her structure, he did not find all her attributes. She managed to keep hidden her ability to eavesdrop on thoughts. Now she knew what he was planning. She could now use that knowledge to gain his trust. She was beginning to regain her warm colour again.

He fiddled about with his spell book shaking his head and flipping pages until he finally stopped and considered a page carefully.

Lifting his head from the page, he studied her briefly before returning to his reading. Finally deciding on his path, Draig waved his hand in a spiralling motion and repeated some chants.

The Halopod felt more stretching, and when she looked down she saw a small bud growing on either side of her body. The buds extended to form small arms. They then expanded into muscular crab like appendages. She hated them already.

Satisfied with his workmanship, Draig then magically and secretly attached the invisible dragline to her new arm. She was ready for her first test of loyalty.

He proceeded to remove the aura cage from around her.

She was suddenly able to focus on things without everything looking blurred. She lifted herself up into the air without feeling any noticeable drag from the gossamer line. She thought now would be a good time to begin manipulation of her captor.

"Oh thank you Master Draig. You do not know how good it feels to be free. I will do anything you want me to do. You are my new master."

He studied her again. She had not immediately tried to instantly vanish, which he knew she could. This was a positive sign. He was certain that she did not know about the concealed dragline. She had passed her first test.

He ignored her antics as she flew around the room enjoying her newly found freedom. She was not going anywhere. He had more important things to consider.

He had studied the Words of all three prophesies.

He had the Stone of Deliverance. That was an essential strategic advantage. Megan was the chosen one. It was through her that the power of The Stone would be released. He needed to share that power. She needed to be persuaded to join with him so that when the power was released it would also infuse into him, thus increasing his power mightily.

Surely his possession of the catalyst would be enough to convince her to share the booty. Without it, she would get nothing. Then, there was the Halopod. She loved the little imp. If she wanted to see it alive again, she would have to acquiesce to his demands. He felt satisfied that he had the upper hand.

* * *

Quan was tossing and turning in his bed in the hay loft of the stable. He preferred to sleep in rough surroundings as he did not want to become soft. He was beside himself with guilt and remorse. He could not just sit by and idly do nothing when The Stone was not in his possession. He had been given a great responsibility when he was made 'The Bearer of the Stone' and he took his title seriously. He was certain that Draig had the relic. He had thought that when they went to the Hajus Woods he would have opportunity to recover his charge. As it turned out, the black Zaurlock had fled. When they arrived at his cave in the woods he had already gone. A thorough search returned nothing.

The Gimp was going to do something. He could no longer wait, and it had to be now. He got up out of bed and quickly dressed. He lowered himself down the ladder from the loft and stood adjusting his clothes in front of his donkey's stall.

"Have you got a plan?"

Quan jumped, but knew straight away that it was his donkey that was projecting its thoughts into his mind.

He answered in Eastlander tongue unsure if the animal could understand. "When did you learn to do that?"

"The fox taught me just yesterday."

Quan was amazed but accepted it quickly. He knew that the Eastlands realm was now full of magic and there was not much that could really surprise him lately.

"And you can understand Eastlander tongue."

"Of course, I have done so for years."

Quan took a quick look around. To an unsuspecting onlooker he would appear to be talking to himself.

All was clear, so he proceeded to saddle his newly gifted

companion.

"My question again. Have you got a plan?"

"Well I am going to Mount Isnar to retrieve The Stone from Draig the black Zaurlock."

"He's a little out of your league isn't he?"

"I am not afraid. Anything would be better than just sitting here doing nothing." Quan's voice took on an impassioned tone.

"You might try this." The donkey shook its head and out of its remaining ear dropped a small black bauble.

Quan leant down and picked up the stone. He jolted his head in surprise. It looked like The Stone of Deliverance.

"Where? How?

"Do not be too quick to presume. The bauble is not the real Stone." The donkey stood waiting for him to ask the next obvious question.

"Where did you come by this?"

"I made it." He went on to explain that when Quan had placed the real Stone in his ear it was putting his balance out, so he used his own magic to make a similar one to fit in his other ear to even things up.

"Well, what is your plan then?" Quan had gained a new respect for his unassuming mount and was willing to consider what the donkey had to say.

The donkey explained that it would be wise to allow Draig to continue to believe that he held The Stone. Even the real Stone would not release its power unless it was in the hand of the chosen one. So he would not become suspicious if a replacement did not do anything extraordinary. It would be a simple matter of exchanging the real one with the one that Quan held in his hand.

Quan was speechless. He had been a fearsome warrior trained in the art of war for decades, and here was a so called dumb animal coming up with a simple but brilliant plan. He now had a new secret and surprisingly smart partner.

"Well?"

"Let's leave immediately." Quan was invigorated, and could not wait to be one their way.

They travelled through the late night hours to Mount Isnar. Negotiating the slippery mountain tracks successfully in the dark they arrived at the tree line just outside the Zaurlock's cave. There was no sign of any activity coming from within. They noticed a gaping hole in one of the sides of his cave.

As Quan was about to come out from behind the tree he froze on the spot, as a group of shadowy figures passed by on silent patrol.

He remembered them from his two previous encounters. They were Draig's recruits from the underworld. He recognized their grinning faces and legless bodies.

He eased his way out once more, signalling his donkey to keep watch.

He crept up to the gap in the cave wall. Edging his way around the opening, he viewed the interior of the cave. It appeared to be empty. He moved further in until his whole body was inside. He was about to begin his search when he noticed Draig laying face down in one of his spell books. He appeared to be fast asleep.

Creeping quietly closer to the sleeping Zaurlock, he almost gave himself away as he tripped against a pot which was on the floor, and obscured from his view in the dim candlelight. Again he froze, not moving a muscle. His hand resting on his dagger.

He happened to glance up and noticed a strange looking being floating near the cave ceiling. The fading candlelight was just bright enough to make the being visible. It was small, about the size of a pear and was quite gruesome looking with huge outsized eyebrows and really muscular arms, which looked out of place on the small body.

He did not move from his position as the being floated down near his face. He thought it was one of Draig's lookouts and that he was about to be discovered.

It did not sound an alarm, but seemed more intent on communicating something to him. It moved down close to the lower section of Draig's robes and used one of the fingers on its little hands to point. It seemed to know that he was looking for something. Could this be an ally in his quest to recover The Stone?

He moved gingerly closer to the sleeping Zaurlock. Deftly he put his hand into the folds of his robe. Draig stirred causing Quan to stiffen. He drew his dagger in readiness. The Zaurlock groaned and repositioned his body with Quan's searching hand moving along with him. He carefully felt for The Stone and was rewarded as he grasped it in his hand. He removed it gradually, and with as much care and stealth as he could muster, he replaced it with the replica.

The little being nodded her approval and went silently back to her original position on the ceiling.

Quan stole his way back out to the gaping hole and was just about to step out into the night, when another group of phantoms glided by, rotating their grinning skulls as they went. He drew back until they had passed, before stepping out into the open moonlit space between the cave and the forest trees. He hurriedly crossed the space and disappeared in to the forest where his donkey waited.

They made their way down the mountain and headed for the palace.

Quan was deeply relieved and grateful to have The Stone back in his possession. He would not let it out of his sight again.

* * *

She had endured much in her life. Her mother had been taken when she was still very young. She had been morphed in to a fox, and morphed yet again into a black panther, and then tortured.

All this she could withstand but the rejection by her father was worse than anything else she had to endure. She loved him, and she thought that he loved her. In her heart of hearts she still knew that he cared. But the rawness of his words and the memory of the look of abhorrence on his face were burning up her emotions.

She wanted to understand why he had reacted like that. How would she like it if he was a morphed into a panther? He had lost her mother and now he thought had lost his daughter. Perhaps he had. She had no way of knowing whether she would ever be human again. He had been a tower of strength since her mother had died. They had enjoyed a closer relationship because they had supported each other in their grief.

Her heart wrenched with a longing that only he could fill. She tried to cry, but her anatomy would not allow it. It only added to her despair. Her sinewy frame dropped to the floor. Placing her paws over her eyes, she tried to block out the world. Was there no relief from this feeling of desolation and longing?

She did not want the responsibility of saving the world. She was just a little girl who wanted her father to tell her that he loved her. Why was she set aside to be the chosen one? Surely there was someone more suited and more capable than her.

She knew that she was feeling sorry for herself, but she did not care. She could not leave the palace for fear that someone would slay her as a wild beast, or Draig would try to abduct her again. This was just as much a prison as Draig's gilded cage had been.

She could not even go to her own room anymore. Not that it would be such a good idea. Each time lately that she tried to sleep there, she was either morphed into an animal or disassembled and sucked out through the ether. What had become of her blissful existence with the long afternoons of adventure and play, living under the bright light of her father's love and affection?

She sat up and tried to lift her own spirits. She was never one to stay down for long. Her mother had always said that about her. She would honour her mother's words and try to see the positives in her dismal situation. There was no benefit in continuing her self pity. It would not change the situation.

She prayed to the Holy One for strength and encouragement, but she knew that she must first start to lift her own spirits. Why was her mother not here when she needed her most?

* * *

My chosen one will be returned to the embrace of her forebear.

Henrik sat in the same chair that he had, when Megan was brought to him. Beside him on the sideboard, lay the necklace, and locket, and the scroll of prophecies.

He had not been to court for days, and everyone was concerned. Even when his queen had died, he still managed to put in a brief appearance at court.

For the first time in his life he could not shake the black feelings, which haunted his every waking hour. Not that he had slept particularly well. He was constantly jolted out of his sleep with nightmares of ghosts, and wild animals attacking him. He was miserable.

The single candle in the room was burned down almost to the point of extinguishing. It flickered, but did not go out. He looked at it, not really seeing it. His hand was on his brow and his eyes slowly closed.

"Henrik my love."

He came to wakefulness with a start and leaned forward in

his chair. He could not believe his eyes. He knuckled them with his hands and looked again his eyes wide.

An apparition of his dead wife stood before him. She was just as he remembered. The fine skin on her face shone with a luminous glow. Her long thick jet black hair hung to her shoulders in soft waves. Her eyes were captivating. She wore a long white robe which looked weightless and it moved as if a light breeze was touching it. Her smile was full showing straight white teeth. She was beautiful. He could not speak, but just continued to look at her.

"Do not be afraid my love. I come only because the need is so great. Our daughter despairs. She has been given great responsibilities and she needs you to love and accept her as she is. Do not despair yourself for how things are now for they will change.

"The answer is within your grasp. Look beside you. The scroll of the three prophesies hold the key. Read them and understand. She is the chosen one. Have faith that the Holy One will not leave her or forsake her, nor should you.

"The prophesy speaks of the Day of Restoration. She will be restored. Be there for her now. Now is when she needs you the most. Have courage my husband, and love our daughter."

He had not moved since she began to speak. He felt like a great heavy weight had been lifted from him. His mind cleared, and for the first time in days he felt like his old self once more.

He was about to say something to his wife when she lifted her finger to her lips in a hushing action. He did not speak.

She looked lovingly into his eyes as she faded from his sight.

He fell to his knees and prayed to the Holy One in thankfulness and gratitude for his own restoration. He vowed to reignite his father love for Megan and support her to the end.

Chapter 16

Henrik had fallen into a deep dreamless sleep following the appearance of his Queen. He had not slept so soundly in many weeks. Before he slept he had read carefully the scroll of three prophecies. He now much more clearly understood their meaning.

A sense of refreshment and peace in his heart greeted him as he awoke early. He now wanted to share that peace with his daughter.

He went to the room which had been set aside for her. He knocked gently at the door. Realizing that Megan could not answer, he opened the door slowly.

Megan's keen senses had heard, and smelled him, long before he had knocked.

She sat regally in wait for him. She did not know what to expect. Was he going to continue his previous hurtful attitude? She had mentally prepared herself for the worst.

He slid his head around the door and looked at her. She could sense immediately the softness emanating from him.

"May I come in?" he smiled at her as he spoke.

She could not answer him, but she could nod her head. He picked up on the sign and came fully into the room. There was a chair in one corner, and he pointed to it, and asked if he could sit.

She nodded again and he sat down opposite her.

"I do not know where, or how to begin, but to say how sorry I am for the beastly way I have treated you." He then suddenly realized how he had phrased the apology, and quickly tried to patch it up.

"I … I did not mean … you were a beast; it is I who has behaved like an animal. Please forgive me."

She found that she was amused at his bumbling apology, but fortunately, it could not show on her feline face. In a way she was enjoying having her father bow and scrape. Now it was her turn to chastise herself for being beastly. There was no place here for amusement, he was mending bridges, and she was very happy about it. She had her father back. She felt whole again. Her heart lifted with the sense of relief she felt. There was no love like a father's love, and she had missed it so much.

She stood up and started to walk toward him. He drew back a little, still feeling some apprehension as he had had no feedback on how she was receiving his olive branch.

She was again bemused at the slightly afraid look on his face. It did not hurt him to have a healthy respect for her. She had to stop herself again, and remind herself that this was a very serious matter.

As she drew closer, she tried to soften her expression to help reassure him. As he did not change his own expression, she decided that it was not working. He would just have to work it out.

He swallowed hard when her face came within his breathing space, but to his credit, he did not flinch or turn away.

He gently took her head in his open hands. She almost melted at his touch. He looked straight into her dark green eyes. His hands fondled her ears as he spoke.

"Megan, I will support and love you, no matter what. You will always be my beloved daughter, and nothing will ever come between us again. I have read the prophesies and you are the chosen one. We have a monumental task to achieve, and I will be there with you every step of the way. I know that you can hear and understand what I am saying to you." He paused, and continued to look lovingly at her. She noticed the brimming up of tears in his eyes.

They were reconciled. He was her father again, she was his daughter. To Megan, the world was back on its axis.

Now she could truly be the chosen one.

* * *

He shook the white Zaurlock roughly by the shoulder rousing him out of his slumber. "Nah wake up quickly." Quan was excited, and wanted to share his excitement with his friend.

Sagent Nah rubbed his bleary eyes, and tried to push his friend away. As he had just that moment awoken, he was not yet fully functioning.

"What can be so important at this early hour Quan?"

"I have The Stone."

Nah was instantly alert. He leapt out of bed and grabbed his short companion by the shoulders.

"Are you certain?" Without waiting for confirmation he continued in his own growing excitement, "Tell me, how did you manage it?"

"It was all the donkey's idea." Quan kept a straight face.

Nah stood straightening his back. A quizzical look framed his face. He thought his little friend had perhaps gone insane overnight.

"Are you serious?"

"On my honour as a warrior, the donkey spoke to me, and hatched a brilliant plan, which we implemented last night while you were sleeping."

Nah still was not convinced.

Quan had pledged not to let The Stone out of his possession. He opened his hand and produced the relic.

Nah looked hard at the artefact, and then sat back on his bed.

"Well, we have the advantage back. Now we can truly plan for the Day of Deliverance." He smiled in genuine relief, nodding encouragement to his friend.

"You have chosen your donkey well Quan. He is just like you, unassuming but brilliant."

Quan beamed at the praise. It was the way he desired people should view him, and his donkey now fitted perfectly. But he was mindful again, as he looked down at The Stone, not to become complacent. The ruse was in place, but they were dealing with a shrewd and conniving enemy, and he was not to be underestimated.

Quan related the full details of the last night's events,

including the sighting of more of the phantoms patrolling outside Draig's cave.

They must prepare, and prepare well. Much depended on the success on that day. The rent in the shroud would only get bigger, and more evil would seep from the underworld, unless it was halted. They had to win, and win decisively.

It was obvious that Draig was recruiting those phantom fiends from below, as there were more of them now being sighted. This had to mean that they were pouring unchecked out of the orifice to the underworld. The numbers would only increase, as this was their only opportunity in centuries to be free from their eternal misery.

They would take over the world if they were not stopped.

It was time to meet with King Henrik and make plans.

* * *

"No, you fool; I said at least two hundred!" Draig spat venom at the head Heinion. He had begun to sway nervously back and forth as it reported his progress. "And stop that infernal swaying."

"But Master Draig, the gateway to the underworld is still restricted and small. Only a few of us at a time can pass through. I am doing my best to secure each one as they come."

"No More excuses. I want two hundred of your best here and ready to do battle by tomorrow night, or I will sear the flesh from your body. Now get out." Draig shouted as he pointed to the solid rock wall, indicating to his ghostly commander the shortest departure route.

The Heinion took one look at the Searing Twitch sitting on Draig's desk and obliged willingly. It quickly exited sideways through the rock wall, nodding its grinning skull as it went.

"Those fools are such a disappointment Halopod." He cooled down as he looked up at newest confidant. He had found the Halopod to be an excellent listener, who rarely disagreed with his judgment.

Gemma descended down to position herself at his eye level, which she now did when he regularly wanted to talk.

"We need to prepare for the Day of Deliverance. That idealistic Megan wants to save the world, by closing the pit. We will let her think that she can succeed, and not dampen her enthusiasm, otherwise she will not come on the day."

She focused on him, giving him her full attention. He liked her to do that. She had not tried to flee, which had helped to build his trust. The changes that he had made to her appearance also helped. It made it easier for him to believe that she had changed inside, as she looked so grim on the outside. She still had not been game to look at herself in a mirror.

He produced the false stone from under his robes.

"This tiny bauble is the key, little imp." He rolled it around in his fingers, over and over as he spoke.

"This is the bait, with which, we will catch the prize. The ultimate measure of power, which will make me the most powerful Zaurlock who ever walked the earth." His eyes shone with a glint of madness, as he let his imagination run unchecked.

She kept her face impassive and attentive. She had the ability to block even the black Zaurlock from harvesting her thoughts. Secretly she thought he was insane. She knew that The Stone was now safe with Quan the Gimp. It gave her a small measure of satisfaction to know, that she had helped orchestrate the ruse. That was the whole reason why she had chosen to remain, and not try to escape from Draig.

"She must be made to share the power. She will never do it willingly. Surely she realizes that now I am the 'Bearer of the Stone.' The one I have read about in the prophecies. This must give me some standing."

Gemma just nodded in agreement. Whatever makes you happy, she secretly thought.

He had become absorbed in his own imaginings. His eyes glazed over in a confused mania. Forgetting her presence he started to rave about how he would spring his trap unexpectedly on the day. They would not be ready for the invasion of fiends that would gush forth, adding to his strength and honouring him as conqueror. Fire would be his weapon, and he would prevail over his enemies. The cat would be destroyed along with his meddlesome brother and his cohorts. Henrik would bow to him in humble adoration.

Not wanting to hear his maniacal ravings, she quietly slipped away into another part of the cave. Nor did she want to be around when he came back to his senses. He would not want her to overhear his dastardly intentions and he would react badly to her presence.

* * *

King Henrik smiled as he strolled proudly through the palace grounds. By his side a huge black panther walked leisurely along. A jewel studded leather leash was attached to a golden collar around her neck. Her black coat shone in the morning sunshine, as though it had just had a thorough brushing. Her chiselled shoulder blades moved up and down with each step, as she padded confidently beside him. From time to time, she turned her head up to him and made eye contact. He winked back at her in response.

Passersby looked frighteningly at the large cat, which made Henrik smile even more.

He had decided to redesign his red battle ensign, to show a black panther leaping forward aggressively with its claws extended, and an angry snarl on its lips. He thought it would honour his daughter, and it would also demonstrate his new found aggression and will to conquer.

He had surprised himself with how quickly he had adapted to his daughters animal form. Although she could not communicate directly with him, they had developed a set of physical signals and other forms of body language, which made for a primitive common understanding between them.

It was a matter of the heart, not the physical that determined their growing relationship. Despite the constraints, they had, in the short space of time, developed a closer bond than they had when she was a ten year old human child. Her new maturity caused him to react differently to her, and they both grew closer because of it. She had always loved him, but she now felt a greater connection to her father. He had overcome extraordinary barriers to make their unusual relationship work, and she respected his efforts and devotion to her.

He had shared with her his supernatural episode where her mother had visited him. Megan was overcome with emotion as he related her mother's words back to her. It was, as if she had heard her cry for help, and leapt across the realms to come to her aid. She missed her mother even more. She consoled herself that at least she still had her father in the here and now. She looked up at him again, and she felt the love for him well up in her heart afresh.

Their morning stroll was interrupted by the sound of a voice calling them.

Sagent Nah came out into the courtyard, waved to get their attention and then called loudly to them.

"Majesty, can we please have some time, it is important."

The king returned his wave acknowledging that he would come immediately. He looked at Megan and saw that she also understood. They moved quickly to where Nah was standing.

"Majesty, we need to have an urgent council of war." He lowered his voice and continued, "We have secured The Stone."

Henrik frowned considering Nah's statement. His hand slipped unconsciously to Megan's nape, and he stroked her as he replied.

"Good work Nah. Let us now plan our strategy."

They walked back into the palace and went directly to the war room, where Rasita and Quan were already waiting. The king's Generals were also there.

Once they were seated Nah began his address.

"I believe that the Day of Deliverance is coming very soon. You have all read the three prophecies. I will paraphrase. The sign of its beginning will firstly be when the Day of Drawing comes. We will all be inexorably drawn to the Valley of Bones to assemble in readiness for the battle, which will take place on The Plains of Rescuse. I believe that Draig and his forces will also be drawn there supernaturally."

The Generals looked solemnly at each other. All were fixated on his every word.

"The rent in the Shroud between the two earths lies somewhere on the Plain of Rescuse. Even now, evil oozes forth unabated out of the pit and into our world. We have a holy mandate to halt the invasion of evil. Megan is the chosen one, to which The Stone will be given, on the Day of Deliverance. With that investiture, great power will be released to make right that which is wrong.

We will assemble our great army to engage and defeat the scourge, which threatens to invade our land. These fiends can be killed. We have, with our own hands slain them in battle. We will completely rout the enemy, disempowering the abductor and rebel, Draig, the black Zaurlock. The king will have his retribution for the personal attack upon his daughter, and his realm."

The Generals raised their fists and their voices, in salute of the rousing words spoken with such passion by the Chief Court Zaurlock.

"Draig is the victim of a clever ruse. He believes that he has possession of The Stone of Deliverance, and that he will have the upper hand on the day of the battle. He is wrong. He is deceived. We hold the real artefact in our possession, and we have the chosen one."

"He is still not to be taken lightly. He has sought to bring evil into our land. He has consorted with the evil one, and I believe he has bargained our freedom for his own relentless quest for more power.

We need now to fully prepare. We do not know the exact time that we will be drawn to the battlefront. The Holy One has His designated time, but we must be ready to move out at short notice."

There was not much more to add to Nah's summation.

They left the war room and went to begin preparations for the Day of Drawing.

Chapter 17

King Henrik, Sagent Nah, Megan, Quan and Rasita had all felt the unquestionable pull at the same time. The Day of Drawing had begun.

Soldiers had been readying themselves for weeks. They were prepared and able to move out in under a day's notice. It was too long since they had been to war, and the men were champing at the bit for some real conflict.

King Henrik called for an emergency session of court. He stood and addressed the assembly.

"We are in a state of war. Today we will dispatch our forces to assemble in The Valley of Bones. We have a holy mandate to go forth and conquer the wrongdoers, and put to the sword any who resist us. We fly the ensign of the black panther. It is ordained by the Holy One. Too long has the rebel Draig had free rein to do as he pleases. He will be brought to heel, and his power will be no more."

He paused before addressing them further.

"My very own daughter is the chosen one. It will be she, who is to release the holy power, which rights the wrong. I pay tribute to my princess Megan."

A cheer arose from the assembly.

"We leave within the hour. This battle is for the sovereignty of our land, and we will not fail."

He was now a man on a holy mission. He dismissed the court and went to the war room to make final preparations.

* * *

The Day of Drawing is coming when My best will be made to be together to defend right on the Plains of Rescuse.

The ten thousand strong army of King Henrik had travelled for two days to reach the Valley of Bones. They were camped just this side of the Plains of Rescuse. From there it was an easy manoeuvre for the full force to be right in the heart of the battlefield.

They were ready and waiting for the command to attack. The many hundreds of battle ensigns fluttering in the wind displayed the black panther boldly. Spirits were high. They had the advantage, and they were going to be ruthless in applying it to the enemy. Every soldier had a personal interest in securing the land for their wives and children.

* * *

Draig felt the pull strongly. He stopped what he was doing, and made sure he clearly understood what was occurring.

"Ah! At last!" He looked around the room seeking his confidant. When he spied her he said, "My little imp, the time has come; the Day of Drawing has arrived."

The Halopod floated submissively down to where he was, and gave him her full attention.

"Go and bring that so called commander of mine to me as fast as you can." He consciously removed the gossamer drag line from her, unless she went too far looking for the Heinion and hit the jarring extent of it. He had come to trust her lately.

She flashed away and was back almost instantaneously, having completed her assignment.

Shortly after the head Heinion wafted through into the cave.

"Yes Master Draig, what can I do for you?"

Draig gave him a withering glare, and said without much enthusiasm.

"Have you managed to organize the two hundred Heinions which I asked you to do for me urgently?"

"Almost Master Draig. We have one hundred and ninety including us six, so far."

Draig rolled his eyes and shook his head. He was only just controlling his rising anger and intolerance for the bumbling minion.

"But master I have good news."

"Do you really? Indulge me Heinion."

It was, as if by some extraordinary coincidence, that the timing of what the Heinion shared was of vital strategic importance to Draig.

"There are many thousands of my fellow Heinions ready to come out of the pit in the next day, and more are preparing as we speak." The Heinion blinked his bright red eyes in anticipation.

Draig jumped up with such gusto, that the Heinion shrank back in fear of reprisal from his angry master. He covered his face in self defence with his bony three fingered hands.

"You have excellent timing, and to think that I was considering replacing you."

Draig now had the missing factor to his plan for battle. He pictured thousands of these fearsome fiends at his disposal, ready to attack at his command.

"Heinion, prepare two hundred recruits for battle. They will be my personal guard."

The Day of Drawing was certainly here, and his new influx of troops was not a moment too soon. He could feel the pull even stronger now.

He must move his forces closer to the pit, where his legions of Heinions would emerge. The Plains of Rescuse was where he would make his future secure.

He was feeling good now. Very good. He rolled the stone between his fingers, feeling the assurance of having the means to immense power in his possession.

* * *

Draig was ready. He sat down into the wickerwork throne and tried it for fit. His arms were draped over the generous arm rests. The throne was fixed to a large circular wooden platform with extended handles spiralling out at every arms length around its perimeter.

"Yes it will do nicely." He stood, and motioned to the Heinion soldiers to have the structure taken outside, as they would be leaving immediately. The day was passing and he wanted to be at the site before it drew completely to a close. He wanted to be early for the Day of Deliverance, which would surely be the very next morning.

He looked like a warrior. All seven feet of his height was clad in full battle dress. His black leather suit fitted his large muscular body snugly. The armoured shoulder protection broadened his already wide frame. Long knee length snake skin boots donned his feet. Tight fitting leather gloves covered his bony hands. The wide leather belt held his twitch and his curved dagger. His dark shoulder length hair was slicked back with oil. The shaggy beard had been trimmed to short stubble. He had, for the occasion, magically inscribed heavy black finger width runes on his face from beneath his eyes running diagonally to his cheek bones. A single heavy gold neck chain fell almost to his navel. The small pouch holding the stone was tied to the golden chain. The rest of his arsenal was within him. He had spent the entire night charging himself with every conceivable shard of magic he could conjure. As agent for the evil one he had asked for a special dispensation of power and influence for the event. The sensation of supremacy and command enveloped and permeated his entire being. He was ready.

Two hundred Heinions had gathered outside the cave on Mount Isnar. The milled around in loose formation waiting for further orders from Master Draig.

In the fading afternoon light he appeared from the large gap in his wall. As he stepped out to face his contingent of Heinion soldiers, he loosed a series of explosive fireworks, which rocketed skyward, just to make his first impression on the troops memorable.

They lit up the skies above Mount Isnar and filled the air with their acrid burnt smell.

His little demonstration over, he walked regally out through the smoke filled air and down to where his mounted throne sat among the ranks of soldiers.

He sat down on the throne, purposely taking his time. The Halopod came and floated obediently over his right shoulder. Her small face had also been marked in black runes similar to her master's. She noticed that he absently, and without looking at her, reattached the invisible gossamer dragline to her arm.

He raised his voice and yelled his throaty order. "Now lift me into the skies and take me to the battlefield."

They gathered around his throne like hungry hordes, gaining purchase where they could on the multiple handles. The scene looked like worms in a bucket moving and twisting, as they fought for position. As the obstreperous throng started to sway their lower bodies in unison, the platform began to rise. As it gradually gained height, other Heinions moved in under it and added their swaying to the uplift. Those that could not touch the structure directly formed a long dragon like tail, which trailed behind swaying from side to side, in a long undulating motion. The dying rays of sunlight reflected off the hundreds of shiny Heinion skulls, giving the tail a resplendent effect. It was truly mystical to behold. Each one of the ghostly swaying cohort started to chant and sing their battle song of triumph.

The black Zaurlock sat back and relaxed, as the whole structure rose majestically into the air. It reached a height far above the ground before it started to move off in the direction of the Valley of Bones.

* * *

It was almost nightfall on the Day of Drawing, as King Henrik and Megan walked down the middle of the rows of soldiers standing at attention. The two rows faced each other, as they waited for their inspection. Sagent Nah, Quan and Rasita, followed the King and the panther.

They were about halfway down the long rank, when one of the soldiers yelled a warning, and pointed skyward.

Every eye turned upward to see what it was that had drawn his attention.

Streaking across the sky in the orange sunset was what looked like a huge dragon. It was silhouetted against the setting sun, and moving at an impossibly fast rate. A mournful sound accompanied the juggernaut, as hundreds of male phantom voices chanted their eerie song. The voices melded into a constant drone. They had never seen anything like it before.

Nah activated his ether vision and drew the image closer to him. He immediately recognized his brother, sitting on a throne. His head was back, and he had his hands raised in the air. The structure was supported and powered by what looked like hundreds of swaying phantoms, stretching out to form the long tail.

The soldiers began to break ranks in panic. Nah held up his

hands to quell the nervous men, and then told them exactly what, and who it was.

Nah reluctantly admired his brother's style, and thought to himself, that he certainly knew how make an entrance.

The fiery pseudo dragon disappeared over the hills which surrounded the Valley of Bones, and no one was in doubt, about where Draig and his minions were heading.

* * *

Draig was overjoyed. Here he was flying through the air on his way to the greatest victory in his life. The cool evening air was buffeting against his face and rushing through his hair. He had never felt such ecstasy and thrill. It was not just the external blissful feeling he was experiencing. He was charged full with magic. It all but oozed out of him, causing him to experience a most rapturous and euphoric rush of pleasure. The host of rhapsodic male chanting voices added to his feeling of elation. Surely he was reaching his Zenith.

As he passed over the Valley of Bones, he looked down and noticed two long lines of what looked like soldiers. He thought to himself, that it must have been Henrik's army. Fools. His plan did not involve having to waste effort dealing with them. He was too smart to risk his unknown and untested group of half carcasses against those battle hardened thugs.

It was almost time. He closed his eyes and enjoyed the ride.

Chapter 18

The breaking dawn ushered in The Day of Deliverance. The air was crisp and fresh. It started in similar fashion to most other days, but would finish very much different to any other. This day would determine how the course of rulers would run. The clash of good and evil would yield a winner, and a loser. There was no grey area in between. If evil prevailed, then the earth would change and become irrevocably worsened. If good won the day, then life could return to normal and honest people could live their lives in peace and prosperity, and their children would be safe.

It was time. King Henrik was magnificently clad in his king's amour. His battle crown was upon his head. His two handed sword sat sheathed in its jewelled scabbard. Megan and Henrik walked together up to the chariot, which had been specially made for them to lead their righteous army into battle. She looked as regal as her father, as she padded her way to where the chariot was waiting. They stepped up into it, and took their places side by side. A ledge had been fixed in place inside the front of the war cart for Megan to put her front paws, allowing her to stand erect. Standing on her back legs, she stood almost as tall as her father.

The outer walls of the chariot were heavily fortified, and had sharpened shafts of metal studding the surface. The wheels were larger than usual, and had maceheads protruding horizontally from the axles. A large red battle ensign was mounted high at the rear, and fluttered in the wind, displaying the emblem of the leaping black panther prominently. Two massive powerfully built white steeds were hitched to the front, either side of the heavy wooden draw shaft of the chariot. They tossed their great heads, flaring their snorting nostrils, and stamping their hooves, impatiently waiting for the battle to begin.

Sagent Nah adorned in full white battle dress rode up on his grey warhorse, and took his place just behind the chariot. The Bearer of the Stone, Quan the Gimp joined him, mounted on his one eared donkey. Rasita leapt up onto the step up at the rear of the Megan's chariot. A line of six specially selected palace guards, and the two escorts from Alabasteil came next. The ranks of mounted lancers formed the rear guard, and they were followed by thousands of foot soldiers, brandishing their weapons. A sea of red battle ensigns rippled challengingly in the wind. They looked a formidable force.

A trumpet sounded loudly signalling the army to begin its march. They moved out in formation. The loud clatter of tack, hooves and weaponry added to the fearsome image of a well disciplined army. The repetitive sound of drum beats set the rhythm for the foot soldiers.

One short march and they would be on the Plains of Rescuse, and into the arena of battle. They were marching to meet their destiny, with a holy mandate fuelling their spirits.

* * *

Draig was also prepared. On the Plains of Rescuse he had positioned himself just adjacent to the rent in the shroud. He knew that his legions of reinforcements would come pouring forth out of the pit at his command. He wanted to reserve that action for the most effective time, and cause the enemy to quake at the sight. He was a master at intimidation, and this stroke of brilliance was going to work exceptionally well.

He sat on his throne facing the Valley of Bones. He had purposefully chosen to bring a throne, as it sent a message to his opponents. He was going to be the new ruler after today.

From this position, he would see the enemy approaching. He could also see the pit. He looked over at the heaving retching quagmire. It seemed to move of its own volition. Snaking along, like an elongated scar in the landscape. It bubbled and gurgled occasionally, spitting spume of sulphur smelling liquid out of the ugly gash and into the air. A heat shimmer rose from it in waves along its length which distorted the view beyond. The rancid smell, and the heat, made it a very undesirable place. He saw the occasional grinning skull pop up, and then disappear again back down into the quagmire of yellow slush. Patience my pretties, patience. Draig smiled at the thought over his plan again. They will not expect my little surprise. His fingers fiddled with the pouch containing the black stone hanging from the gold chain around his neck.

Draig looked behind him. His Heinions had gathered in a mishmash fashion around his throne. They were milling about not really looking like an army at all. Never mind he thought. It mattered not. They could turn nasty when they put their minds to it.

He felt the magical energy pulsating within him, as if it was anxious to be released. The climax was soon to come.

A nervous Heinion squawked in alarm at the first sighting of the human army appearing over the low hill from the Valley of Bones. The royal chariot appeared first as it rose above the horizon. Other blurred figures materialized around it in the shimmering heat.

Soon the entire spine of the hill was dotted with hundreds of soldiers and lancers on horses. The Heinions squirmed and shuffled in response. Some cried out in anguish.

"Silence you fools." Draig raised his hand as he rebuked them fiercely.

They muted their cries bobbing their heads up and down in acquiescence. But some still moved nervously around and looked fearfully at the gathering forces on the hill.

Draig waited. No sign of fear showed on his face. He had a plan.

Gemma the Halopod still floated over his right shoulder. She also saw the approaching army and she was glad. She could actually see Megan even from such a distance away. Her acute vision was another of her innate attributes that allowed her to see clearly over long distances. Her eyes became magnified as she zoomed in on her real mistress.

Megan stood on her hind legs beside her father. Her head was held high and Gemma could see the determination on her feline face. Her black coat shone in the sun. She looked magnificent.

Gemma wanted to flee to her but she remembered the drag line attached to her arm. She would wait until she was closer and then she would go to her.

The army started to increase their speed as they moved down onto the more even area of the sweeping plain. A great cloud of dust arose behind them as they moved as one body across the vast treeless Plain of Rescue.

Draig watched and waited. Not even a flicker of nervousness showed on his impassive face. His hands were casually clasped in front of him.

The army was within striking distance of the enemy now and broke into a full battle charge. The hue and cry of the marauding soldiers rose to fever pitch as they thundered down on the still seated Zaurlock.

They were almost upon him.

He leapt to his feet and raised his hands shouting a hideous incantation at the top of his voice. He clenched his fists and they swelled with the restraining force of the pent up magic. He opened his hands and the diabolism was released in great lightning like tendrils which spiralled and wound there way upward. A huge ball of fire formed above them and, expanding out from its centre it created a massive circular dome of flames. The dome spiralled and rotated as it descended down on them all. The flaming wall of the semi sphere severed a dividing line neatly between all of the charging forces and their leaders separating them and then sealing itself tightly against the hard ground.

The charging soldiers who were left outside hit the impenetrable outer wall of flames. They were repelled back by the heat completely halting their charge. The horses propped digging their rear hooves into the hard ground in an attempt to stop before reaching the flames. Some could not stop and were engulfed in the fire and perished. Others reared and fell back in disarray. Mayhem and confusion was rampant. They could no longer see through the flaming structure in front of them. Their leaders were gone.

Inside the massive fiery dome Draig watched as the charging leaders were forced to slow down and stop. They looked around them in confusion. The environment inside the dome was oddly hushed. After the rush of the charge the atmosphere was by comparison, eerily quiescent and quiet. Only the occasional gurgle coming from the pit disturbed the stillness. There was a strange serenity surrounding them. A holy quiet. Even the Heinions were still. There was no heat coming from the walls of the flaming dome. It was pure magic at work.

Draig sat back down on his throne.

"Welcome to the Day of Deliverance my friends," he spread open his hands showing upturned palms in a mock gesture of greeting.

The pit bubbled and gurgled ominously in the background.

Henrik and his now small band of fighters said nothing. They were now at a clear disadvantage as the Heinions greatly outnumbered them and they were separated from their main force. Megan remained in the chariot beside her father. Sagent Nah, Quan and Rasita had changed their positions to move up beside their leaders. The remaining six palace guards that had made it through into the dome with them stood silently behind with their drawn swords still in their hands.

"Just in case you were thinking of any further aggressive behaviour I would like to show you one more small surprise." He tried unsuccessfully not to look too pompous about his early surprise tactic.

He stood to his feet again and extended both of his hands toward the quagmire bringing them together in an interlocking fist. Power exuded from him in long viscous streams extending all the way to the pit. In response the rent in the shroud opened its gaping tear further and in a regurgitating action it began to spit out slush covered Heinions. It was like a great terrestrial maternal birth canal gushing forth its hideous newborns. The flow smoothed and the legless fiends came gushing out in droves. As they emerged they swayed and wafted their way into the dome and formed random lines behind Draig's throne. The procession continued for some time. Draig sat again but did not watch the flow of minions. He was more interested in watching the reaction on the faces of his band of captives.

They returned his look without showing fear. They could see him seated on his throne as the hordes of fidgeting Heinions gradually built up behind him. He just kept looking at them and gauging their response. He seemed to be enjoying himself immensely. The level of noise was increasing as the size of his army swelled. Eventually the flow stopped. The area behind the throne was filled to capacity. At least three thousand more skulls grinned fiendishly back at them.

Quan dismounted and sidled across to the rear of the chariot. Moving up behind Megan he produced The Stone and placed it reverently between her front paws. She glanced down at the relic and without showing any reaction she looked back up into Draig's eyes. He was still confident. He still thought he had the real Stone.

Gemma the Halopod had been watching Megan ever since she had come into the dome. She knew that her mistress would probably not recognize her with the disfiguring changes he had made to her appearance.

She thought that Draig was on the cusp of doing something dreadful. She may not make it through the skirmish. Now was the time for her to show her true colours and let Megan know that she had not been forsaken or betrayed by her little messenger. Having made her decision she left her position and flew as fast as she could directly toward Megan calling as she went.

"Megan, Megan, it's me Gemma."

Megan saw her coming and immediately recognized her voice. She had no time to wonder why Gemma looked so gruesome. The Halopod was almost to her when she was stopped abruptly in mid flight. It was as if she had hit a glass wall. She smashed hard against the invisible barrier as the gossamer drag line reached the end of its short tether. Gemma fell to the ground stunned but still alive. She bravely tried to float upwards again in an effort to reach Megan but was suddenly hit from behind with the deadly sharp thrust of Draig's dagger. It impaled her small body with its lethal point sending her plummeting back down to the ground. She did not move again.

Draig remained standing in front of his throne. His hand still extended from the lethal strike he had just made. Anger framed his cruel face.

"Little traitor," he spat the words at the dead Halopod lying in front of Megan's chariot. The multitude of Heinions extolled and lauded him with thousands of clattering teeth and rattling swords.

Megan was shocked. Her Gemma was dead. She looked at the inert figure lying on the hard ground – the vicious curved dagger still protruded from her small body. Megan almost gave in to the temptation to move too early and attack the murderous Zaurlock. Her father quickly placed his hand on her front leg. With his other hand he drew her chin to him and looking into her eyes he said forcefully. "Keep your mind on what you must do. Lives depend on it."

It took all her strength to keep herself controlled. She wanted to leap out of the chariot and pounce on him and tear him to pieces.

She did not do it. Her eyes were blazing with the restrained fury she felt.

Draig made sure she saw him smiling.

She looked down at The Stone still sitting between her paws.

In her hand it shall cause the shroud to be restored and evil to once again be contained.

The words resounded in her mind. They had a calming effect on her.

"And now it's time for the grand finale." Draig still standing in front of his throne produced the black bauble which he thought to be the real artefact. He moved his outstretched hand in a wide semi-circle and back again showing off the bauble for all to see.

"With this Princess Megan, the chosen one we will share the power it holds. Come and I will place it in your hand as the prophecy dictates." His eyes glowed with avarice as he started to walk toward her. His lips parted in a devious smile.

She drew her paws together in front of her with The Stone of Deliverance between them. As soon as she made contact with the relic it began to glow with a holy radiance. The intensity increased until refulgent shafts of the supernatural light poured forth in a resplendent display of sheer sanctifying power.

Henrik and Quan were forced back away from her as the power was now flowing unchecked from The Stone. She experienced an amazing feeling of buoyancy and light heartedness which was overwhelming her senses.

Draig was dumbfounded. He could not understand what was happening. He had the Stone, didn't he?

Megan the panther closed her eyes. She was still standing on her hind legs and leaning on the ledge in front of her. Her head was hanging slightly forward. A surge of pure power from the centre of The Stone hit her physical body with an intensity that caused her to throw her head back and wail with the pleasure it gave her. Change began. A metamorphic alteration shook every cell in the panther body. Every eye was fixed on her. They witnessed her transformation before their very eyes.

Princess Megan lifted her head. She was human. She was beautiful. Her long black hair fell to her shoulders in soft waves. Her skin was white and pure like milk and her emerald green eyes shone with vivid intensity. The light from the Stone did not abate but shone brighter lighting up her face like some angelic being. A halo of radiant incandescent light surrounded her face. She was dressed in a long white robe of smooth fabric with no adornments or design. Purity and simplicity exemplified. She raised her hands up level with her eyes and held the glowing Stone in front of her.

"I give you The Stone of Deliverance." She raised it higher above her head. The power surged out and forward from it ploughing forcefully into the ranks of the Heinions. The throng was pushed back by the mighty strength emitted from The Stone. They stumbled over each other in the panic trying to get away from the light. They were caught in their own fiery dome and could not escape. Bodies started to fuse together. The top half of one fiend found the top half of another and they became one melded disfigurement unable to move around freely any longer. Each disabled coupled pair lay thrashing about desperately on the hard ground.

Draig was horrified at the melee that was happening behind him. His forces were becoming useless beings with a head at each end and four flailing arms. He had to act. He raised his hands to cast a mighty spell of destruction.

Megan saw his intention early and brought The Stone around pointing it directly at him. He was immediately held fast and could not move a muscle. An expression of shocked amazement was frozen on his face.

She directed the force emanating from The Stone back to the Heinions.

The last few were being cobbled together. She purposefully swung the Stone around and focused its power on the pit. The rent in the shroud opened up into a large circular funnelled orifice. The disfigured Heinions were systematically sucked up into the air and drawn across in a long stream and dumped unceremoniously into the waiting receptacle. Every last one was taken.

Draig was abandoned and alone. The cataclysm had been averted.

Before releasing him from the physical constraint she disempowered the black Zaurlock by drawing out of him all his dark magic. In the process it was converted into good magic and absorbed into the repository of The Stone. He could move again but was now completely powerless. He sensed his own impotency. He still held the black bauble in his hand. He looked despondently at it and then angrily threw it down onto the hard wooden platform smashing it into a thousand useless shards.

'Thereafter on the Day of Deliverance those who seek and persist in wrong will be banished into the pit'

The Words sounded in the dome. All looked around at the vast ceiling of flame to see where the Words had come from. There was an invisible deity present. Omnipresence pervaded the atmosphere. The Holy One had announced His presence.

Megan looked directly at Draig. He lifted his chin in defiance and spat at her. His eyes filled with hatred. "You will not win, you will …"

"Silence," Megan's voice issued forth the ominous command.

She placed The Stone on the ledge in front of her. Raising her right hand she released the pent up power within her binding his mouth from further speech. His eyes darted from side to side in his confusion as he tried to mouth some obscenity.

Noticing a length of burnt out log lying on the ground near the pit she raised it magically into the air and positioned it behind Draig's shoulders. He looked anxiously at it as it rested against the nape of his neck. His arms were mysteriously forced apart and leather thongs bound his hands. She lifted him off the ground holding her fist like she had him by the scruff of the neck. He opened his mouth to scream as his shoulder joints were wrenched hard but no sound could come forth. He just hung there helplessly. He was a pathetic sight.

Megan's jaw was set in cold resolve. Her eyes impassive. The outworking prophecy overriding any pathos she may have felt for her defeated oppressor.

"Draig the black Zaurlock, you have persisted in wickedness. You have sought to bring evil into this world, to feed your own lust for supremacy. You have bargained the freedom of others, for your own hunger for power. The words of the prophecy have been proclaimed, and now this day, they will be fulfilled."

She moved him across and suspended him high above the centre of the gaping belching pit. The sulphur bubbled and hissed below him, releasing stench filled heat waves which rose and engulfed him. His eyes were still defiant.

She opened her closed fist, and he dropped out of sight, into the foul pit of evil.

Megan placed her hands on The Stone. The rent in the shroud began to fold over itself and close. The belching and gurgling ceased, and all movement finished. It finally closed, completely sealing in the evil underworld and its inhabitants. The air cleared of the rancid stench that had pervaded the dome. The landscape where the rent had been was now just like it had been before. Not a scintilla of the evil remained.

The dome of fire immediately extinguished itself and vanished into the ether letting in the bright sunshine and fresh air. The soldiers, who had completely surrounded the dome, rushed in as it disappeared. Megan passed The Stone back to Quan for safekeeping. Only he, and she, could hold it. Its power still flowed. She walked out of the chariot to where the lifeless form of Gemma lay. She picked up the small disfigured body and removed the deadly weapon that had taken her life. She threw it to the ground. She placed the small body in the folds of her robe, drawing it close to herself. She held her grief, as the legion of soldiers filed in and hedged around her and the king.

It was over. Rasita came to Megan and looked searchingly into her eyes. She reached down and touched his head. He responded by nuzzling her leg. It was the best he could manage. She understood.

Nah embraced her gently, without saying anything. It had been a hugely eventful day, and he sensed her grief at the loss of Gemma.

The close knit group who had experienced the amazing events within the dome wasted no time in leaving the Plains of Rescuse.

The army could follow afterwards.

The sun was setting on The Day of Deliverance, and if they travelled through the night, they could be back at the palace for the rising of the sun on the Day of Restoration.

Chapter 19

It was almost daybreak as the twenty palace guards walked their horses along the ribbon of cobbled road that led up to the moat bridge and the palace gates. The war chariot with the king and his daughter rumbled slowly along close behind them. The red ensign hung sombrely down on the staff on the rear of the war cart. It was as if its job was done and it no longer needed to fly. Nah the white Zaurlock, and Quan the Gimp rode their mounts side by side. Rasita the fox trotted along the walking path beside the road. Another twenty mounted soldiers followed up as rear guard.

They had travelled through the night to be at the palace on the Day of Restoration. The promise of miracles hung on the Words of the prophecy. The Holy One had not failed to fulfil the Words so far, and they were all filled with anticipation and expectation of the wonderful things that would happen this day.

None felt tired, but rather they were exhilarated. Even Megan had delayed the depth her grief about Gemma's death to revel in the growing sense of euphoria that was around in the atmosphere. She looked back at the fox padding along the walking path beside them. Perhaps it was his day for a miracle. She had once said to him that she would do all she could to get him back to his human form. She was feeling that anything was possible this day.

The small troop entered the palace just as the dawn broke in the eastern sky. It was a fine day coming in so many ways, and the weather seemed somehow to know the significance as well, bringing blue skies and gentle breezes. The land was free, everything felt lighter, and different. Evil had been expunged from the Eastlands realm and goodness flowed unabated.

Henrik called the assembly together. For the first time in the realm's history an early morning breakfast feast, combined with the assembly of court was to be held in the palace dining room. Cooks and servants were rushing frantically around preparing food and baking fresh bread for the occasion. With such short notice, they needed a small miracle to be ready on time, but they made it and all was prepared within just a few short hours of the king's arrival.

The dignitaries and people flowed into the royal dining room, and the place was quickly packed to capacity. The mood was festive and the wine flowed early. People could sense the freedom and took the opportunity to revel in it. This was truly a different day.

Megan had gone to one of the guest bedrooms to bathe and freshen up before the feast. She had put Gemma's body, along with the locket, in a small crystal casket which had been used for a jewellery box. She reverently placed it on the sideboard while she dressed. A long, full length mirror sat on the floor in the room. She dressed and brushed her newly acquired thick, wavy black hair until it shone before standing in front of the mirror. She was beautiful and she was grown up.

She looked similar to how she remembered her mother. The same thick black hair was the most significant change to her looks. Was it her mother's genes, or was it something to do with her being morphed into a black panther? She did not entertain any further conjecture on the subject. She was just pleased to be back in human form, and she was not dissatisfied with how she now looked.

It seemed that again she had been saved, and Rasita was still stuck in his fox body. She felt a sense of obligation to him which went beyond just their friendship and similar morphing experience.

She felt love. There, she had admitted it to herself, even though she had not even seen him as a human. What did he look like? She decided that it was of little consequence. She knew his heart, and it was beautiful. They had shared a most unusual experience together, and out of it had grown something special. She hoped that he felt the same way. She put the thoughts of love out of her mind, and finished preparing for the day that many things would change for the better.

* * *

A dais had been set up in front of the king's feasting table. The dining room was filled with over four hundred seated guests. The tables were laden with all manner of food and drink. Minstrels played music and jesters did tricks on the dais to entertain the guests. King Henrik sat centrally at his table. On his right hand sat Princess Megan. A small diamond tiara graced her head. On his left was Sagent Nah. His white beard freshly washed and combed for the occasion. Quan sat next to his friend Nah, displaying his usual stoic demeanour. Other dignitaries filled the remaining seats. King Henrik, dressed in his royal regalia stood to address his assembled people.

"Good people of The Eastlands, we have come through a tumultuous time when evil has savaged our land, and our people. I can declare with confidence this day, that it is finished. The evil Zaurlock Draig has been banished to the pit along with his cohorts."

The people cheered and hooted at his welcome words.

"This is the Day of Restoration according to the prophecy. On this day miracles will happen. Lives will change and be truly restored."

Again the people's voices rose in joyous praise and celebration.

"My daughter Princess Megan has been restored to me." He swept his hand toward her and urged her to rise. She stood, and the people applauded wildly in their joy, both for the king, and for them as the people. She could feel their love pervading her soul. She sat back down and they continued to applaud their new princess.

"My only daughter Princess Megan was the chosen one as proclaimed in the prophecy. It was she who held the Stone of Deliverance and ridded the earth of evil. The rent in the shroud has been sealed."

The people stood to their feet cheering at the news. They would have continued to cheer had not the king raised his hands to quell their overwhelming response.

"Her work is not done yet. This day, she will again take up The Stone and release its power to fulfil the last part of the prophecy. I declare this, The Day of Restoration."

The enthusiastic people went wild with the king's declaration.

"But for now, eat and be merry." He sat down, lifted his tankard of wine to his lips and drank deeply from it.

The feasting continued on until most had eaten and drank their fill. The king wanted this to be a joyous occasion and did not constrain the festivity. But now it was time to be serious. He stood and hushed the conversation. His face looked solemn as he began to speak.

"The time has come for us to witness the acts that will be recorded in the history of the realm as being some of the most extraordinary of all time. Firstly, I as king have a personal debt to repay. An extraordinary young man by the name of Rasita Darilus has, through his selflessness and bravery, been instrumental in saving and restoring my daughter to me, and to you her people. For this, I truly thank him. He has been treated sorely by the forces of evil, and my hope this day is that he will be restored. Bring in Rasita Darilus."

Rasita padded his way past the long rows of people lining the aisle way which led to the dais. The people all looked at him in wonder and confusion. They had expected a man, but this was a common fox walking toward the king's table.

"Do not be alarmed people. This is in order." The king stood, and welcomed the fox to the dais.

Rasita looked up at Megan. She smiled back at him, reassuring him. Under instructions from the king a servant bought a white cloth cover and wrapped it around the fox's torso. It was tied at the front. If he was restored they did not want a naked man in the dining room.

Quan bought The Stone to Megan and gently placed it in front of her on the table. He bowed and went back to his seat. She stood and took the relic in her hands, holding it in front of her.

The people looked on in awe as the magic started to emanate from her hands.

Rasita felt the holy influence all over him like warm oil. He crouched down under the power into an almost foetal position.

His body started to morph; slowly the shape of a man began to form up and emerge. The light intensity increased so much that his body was completely covered, and could not be seen clearly. He was enveloped in a mystical penumbra.

The people were mesmerized and did not make a sound.

As the light abated, Rasita was made whole again. He stood up, looked straight at Megan and smiled. She was speechless. He was very, very handsome. He was tall with broad shoulders and a well muscled torso. His hair was thick and blond falling in tight waves to his jaw line. His friendly blue eyes were only eclipsed by his broad smile. Secretly she was overjoyed, but did not show it. She struggled to keep her mind on the supernatural task before her.

The crowd applauded wildly at the amazing feat of magic which they had just witnessed. Rasita bowed to the king, and to her, and then went from the dais. Now was not the time to show the reaction he felt. He was too overwhelmed, and Megan still had much to do. He could wait. He could still hear the deafening applause coming from the excited people as he left the room.

Megan saw him leave, and understood. She now dearly wanted to bring the power to Gemma. She did not know if what she desired was possible, but she had to believe and have faith that this was truly her Halopod's day as well. She laid the Stone down on the table. The power had filled her. She could feel the pent up force within her. She opened the small crystal casket which lay on the table next to The Stone. The little body looked pathetic as it lay in the padded jewellery box. Draig had really disfigured her little Gemma. The ugly eyebrows and muscular arms did not detract from the feeling that Megan had for her.

She lifted the still, cold body out of the box and held it in her hands. Tears welled up and ran freely down her cheeks. She closed her eyes and prayed to the Holy One. The warm honey like feeling of the power exuded from her hands and into the small body. A slight movement caused Megan to open her eyes. Gemma floated up and hovered in front of her. She was completely and miraculously restored to her original form.

Gemma smiled and looked lovingly at her. "You look beautiful Princess Megan." She floated up and did a swirl in the air in a mock curtsy releasing a stream of sparkles in her wake.

Megan laughed, and all the people joined her as the place erupted again with unfettered joy.

As if on cue, a donkey entered the room and trotted down

the long aisle. It only had one ear, and much to the amusement of the people, he brayed loudly as if to say that he also needed a miracle. He stepped boldly up onto the dais and looked expectantly at Megan

Quan jumped up and waved his finger threateningly at his precocious mount.

Megan laughed along with the others but saw that Quan's disfigured donkey really did need something done with that missing ear.

She moved down onto the dais and approached the lop eared animal. She placed her hand on the round scarred area which was once his ear. Out of the white skin a new ear came budding forth. It grew miraculously and continued to grow until it was actually far too long. Now he looked more lopsided.

The crowd burst into raucous laughter. Megan smiled, and then frowned as she looked at the donkey's newest problem. The ear shrank back to its correct size. Quan flopped back down in his seat relieved.

Many more wonderful miracles happened that day. Droves of people came and were healed and restored. It was truly a Day of Restoration, and it was recorded in the annals of the history of the Eastlands realm as the most extraordinary, and miraculous day ever.

Chapter 20

... and true love will blossom like the fruit tree in season.

It had been their favourite meeting place for many blissful months of their blossoming courtship. Megan and Rasita sat together on the lush green grass under an ancient oak tree in the forest close to the palace. Its large bows reached out over them giving them the feeling of shelter and protection. The sun shone in the blue spring sky and filtered its warming rays through the foliage above them. The dappled pattern made by the shadows of the leaves and the sunshine danced around them. The warm breeze bought with it the feeling of peace and that everything was right with the world. Small birds flitted and dived. Bees hummed in perfect harmony with the day.

So much had happened that this charmed respite from events was truly welcomed by them both. Rasita's heritage and royal blood line had been restored by Megan's father, and he was now a fitting suitor for her. They had no responsibility but only to enjoy each other's company. They just took in the peace and obvious joy and felicity that surrounded them.

She looked at him. The mottled shadows from the leafy canopy above were cast over his face and moved as the wind gently blew in the trees. He was definitely handsome. She was pleased about that. His strong jaw and soft lips were playing havoc with her senses.

She took a deep breath and smiled up at him. He returned her smile, and she again noticed his straight white teeth.

"Rasita, it is so good to finally see you as you really are. It's really you isn't it? I'm still having trouble believing that we are here together." Her eyes sparkled as she spoke to him.

"You have no idea how good this feels for me to be free and to be here with you like this as well." He leaned back with one arm supporting him from behind.

For her, something was absolutely right about it. Something deep inside her awakened. She felt dizzy with pleasure for just a moment.

It felt like she was floating. It was a beautiful feeling just being here with him. She cherished every moment.

She moved closer to him and nestled her head against his strong shoulder, looking lovingly up at him.

"I've written something for you." He reached into his satchel and bought out a scroll.

On it was a poem. He read it to her.

When the dawn kisses the morning my first thoughts are of you
I reach out ... you are there ... warm and close
My arm your head to rest ... intimacy entwines
Love rises in the half-light greeting the new day
How sweet and fresh the feeling ... peace abounds
Time disappears in the presence of each other
Two become one ...
Our senses wrapping the soul in the sweet caress of love ...
Eyes meet and no words are needed for the language of love speaks boldly in silence
Reaching out ... touching ... loving ... our peace complete
Knowing each other ... ever in love's abode we have plumbed its depths together ...
Forever ...

He looked down at her upturned face. Her lips were slightly parted.

Without another word they came together as if they had known each other forever. He kissed her long and hard on the lips. She responded to his touch with a passion that surprised her. She wanted him never to leave. She loved him with all her heart. They held each other tightly. Their arms wrapped around each other in a lover's embrace.

The awkwardness that was there at first completely dissolved in their blossoming passion for each other. They stayed in each other's embrace for a long time, not wanting to part.

The way he was holding her made her realize how much she had wanted him even when they were locked in their morphed state, there was something tangible drawing them together.

Her eyes filled with tears as they finally released each other.

She looked again deeply into his eyes and whispered, "I love you."

He gently touched her cheek with his hand and said, "And I love you with all my heart."

She leaned against him and just allowed herself to get lost in the feeling of being so close to him. She toyed with the locket hanging around her neck as they looked out into the warm sunshine. Many months had passed since the Day of Restoration and there was peace in the Eastlands. Her life had become routine again and she liked it. She was blissfully happy with the ordinary. However, she had not been able to sleep back in her room since she had returned to the palace - too many strange and unusual things happened there.